Those Among Us

By

Daniel Loubier

www.AuthorMikeDarkInk.com

Copyright © 2014 Daniel Loubier.
All Rights Reserved.

ISBN: 978-0-9910330-6-5
Library of Congress Control Number: 2014935012

All rights reserved. No part of this book may be reproduced or transmitted in any form or by any means, electronic or mechanical, including photocopying, recording, or by any information storage and retrieval system, without permission in writing from the publisher or author.

First Published by *AuthorMike Dark Ink*, 8/13/2014

www.AuthorMikeDarkInk.com

AuthorMike Dark Ink and its logo are trademarked by *AuthorMike Ink Publishing*.

Printed in the United States of America

For MJ, the bravest little girl I know.
And for Bailey. Always for Bailey.

The following story was inspired by true events. All names have been changed to protect the identities of those involved.

PROLOGUE

Douglas Mitchell's daughter is haunting him.

Her middle-of-the-night footsteps are tiny thieves that rob him of sleep and steal his precious sanity—intruders in the dark that tear away his perception of everything he once thought was real.

She doesn't do it intentionally; there is no malice behind her actions. In fact, her behavior is quite innocent. But it happens almost every night now, and Doug has come to expect it. It's happened so many times his body has grown used to waking up at this hour.

He can *feel* her get out of bed, even before he hears her. Something inside his subconscious shouts at him, "Wake up!" and he's awake. His wife, Carla, never wakes until Janie is already in their room. Carla doesn't appear to be affected by it like he is. So he just lays there...waiting for the inevitable—the message. The words he's heard umpteen times before, but still hopes every day and every night to never hear again.

It seemed so harmless in the beginning. Janie would come into their room; she would complain of a noise and ask if she could sleep in her parents' bed. Then, either Doug or Carla would get up and walk Janie back into her room. They would promise her there was nothing to be afraid of, and they'd wait until Janie drifted back to sleep before returning to their bedroom.

If only they'd known what was really happening.

When they finally realized what was going on, Doug felt like a bully. All those times he'd encouraged her back into her room, forced her to sleep in her room alone, all the while thinking she was only playing a seven-year-old's game. But it was never a game.

And now Doug lies in bed, eyes wide open, with no company other than his unconscious wife and the terrifying knowledge of what's about to happen.

His heart rate increases, as it does every night around this time. He still hasn't heard Janie get out of bed. He turns his head slowly, careful to silence the friction of his head against the pillow, as if any sudden movement will create a noise—a kind of invitation, even though an invite won't be necessary. He reaches for his cell phone on the nightstand to read the time. It's two-thirty a.m.

He quietly sets the phone down and grabs the comforter with both hands, pulling it closer to his face—a reflex born from his fear. He looks to his right again. Carla is still asleep. He stares at the ceiling and says a silent prayer that this time will be different. He prays that this time Janie will not come into their room, he will get back to sleep, and the next time he wakes up the sun will be out because it will be morning and it will be time for work and school. Time for normal life to resume. Not time to deal with whatever the hell is happening inside their home.

Doug doesn't even notice the empty silence of the house until a few minutes after he's begun to pray, when his prayer is interrupted by thoughts about the next day. In fact, it already *is* the next day; it's just too early to appreciate it yet. Too early to live in the next day. Because right now he has to live *here*. In this moment. At this time. They all do.

Doug hears a small, metallic twang. And then another. That's the sound of the coils under Janie's mattress reacting to the shift in weight. She's getting out of bed. She's right on time.

Doug's breathing has quickened now and matches his heart rate. He looks to his right a third time, but Carla is still sleeping.

Dammit, Carla. Why can't you wake up for this?

Beads of sweat form on his forehead, so he reaches to his face—his other hand still firmly tucked under the comforter because he's too scared to remove both hands from the sheets—and brushes the moisture away from his skin.

Down the hall, the sound of Janie's blanket sliding ominously across her bed is another guarantee of the events that are about to unfold.

Ever since the beginning, Doug's hearing has been acute at this hour and he hears her feet fall softly onto the Berber carpet. Some nights she wears socks to bed, some nights she doesn't. Tonight she's barefoot. How he knows this inane detail is nearly impossible, but he knows.

Her footsteps, though seemingly innocuous and unassuming, are maddening. The very sound of each footfall paralyzes him and pins him harder to the bed. Sometimes he considers getting up, walking out into the hall, and meeting her halfway, but he's too frightened. All these months later, he still hasn't found a way to deal with this.

Janie has reached the hallway now. Doug can tell because her tiny footsteps are no longer soft and muffled; now they slap easily on the hardwood floor and echo gently through the house.

She's much closer now. She's definitely coming into their bedroom tonight.

Doug's right knee is now shaking. It's a nervous tic. He does it unconsciously whenever he feels anxiety. His calves are also taut and he's surprised they haven't contracted into spasm yet. His entire body is rigid, in fact; rigid, yet trembling at the same time.

He can hear Janie's breathing—those light, effortless, calm breaths. It's one of the things that really scares him—that she's *not* as scared as he. It's intimidating. He wishes she would show some kind of emotional reaction—even nervous laughter would help at this point—but it's not going to happen, and Doug knows it. It's almost as if what's been happening in the house is an inconvenience to her rather than something trying to hurt her.

She reaches the doorway to their room. Her heels tap against the edge of the hardwood and her toes sink into the soft carpet of the room. She stops.

Why does she always stop? Is it some kind of preparation?

Doug wonders if it's because Janie knows how terrifying this is for him, and so she pauses to rethink her approach. Maybe she's reconsidering coming into the room at all. Maybe it's something else.

Her feet start moving again. With eyes closed, Doug hears her coming to his side of the bed. She always comes to his side. It's as if whatever it is that inhabits her room *goads* her into coming to Doug, preying on his fear—like when a dog senses fear in a human. Even before it attacks, the dog knows it's already won.

Doug is already defeated. By his own fear. By it. By *him*.

The footsteps close in on the bed. He can feel her presence now. He can feel her breath. He closes his eyes even tighter so she doesn't think he's been awake all this time.

He can see her in the darkness—in the nothing—standing against a black background. She's wearing her pink princess pajamas and holding her blanket—the blue one with the shiny, satin-like surface on one side, and the soft plush on the other. She looks so innocent. She hasn't done anything except stand there and beckon him closer. But he doesn't go to her because he doesn't know what might grab his arm and pull him past her, into the darkness and away from her.

"Daddy?"

Her voice is soft and terrifying. Although he wants to scream, cry, and beg for all of this to stop, he controls himself and doesn't flinch. He doesn't so much as allow his closed eyes to move; even the slightest tremor in his eyelids would reveal to her he's been awake this whole time. By now he has trained himself not to react in such a way. He slowly flutters his eyelids—a practiced maneuver—feigning having just woken up.

"Hey, Sweetie," he says to her. He even fakes a yawn. "Everything okay?"

And then she hits him with the words he's been expecting to hear, but which still dig into his stomach like sharp demon claws, draining his lungs of air and his veins of blood.

"The man is in my room."

Fear bubbles inside him like a volcano ready to erupt, and every ounce of control over his shaking knee and frantic heart is nearly spent. And it's not the fear of her ignorance toward the "man's" intentions by which Doug is taunted. He's not afraid his daughter has been lying to him and Carla

Those Among Us

all this time. He's not afraid she's been playing the "imaginary friend" game a little too long either.

He's afraid because he has seen the man, too.

And he's fairly certain the man has seen him.

CHAPTER 1

It was early November and only a couple weeks away from celebrating Thanksgiving. It was an especially cold fall season—one during which the Mitchells had already begun to employ the use of their coal stove. Carla always joked that coal stoves went out with the Reagan administration—an affable mockery of Doug's old-fashioned nostalgia.

His father had installed a coal-burning stove in the house in which Doug had grown up. Among his father's many rules (don't touch the stove, don't get too close, etc.), he'd always warned Doug and his older brother, Luke, not to add any coal to the stove. Granted, coal heat was cheaper than electric (Doug's parents had baseboard heaters in the 1970s), but coal fuel was still an expense; therefore, his father was the only one allowed to touch the shovel and handle the coal hod, which was a black metal bucket that held the coal. Not to mention coal is also dirty; the last thing Doug's father wanted was to find his sons' hands and clothes covered in coal dust and soot.

The local forecast had reported temperatures in their area would fall into the low thirties, while some of the surrounding "hill" towns—areas situated at higher elevations—would possibly dip as low as the twenties. Before going to bed, Doug set a raging inferno.

"That's not too much coal?" Carla asked.

Doug eyed the stove and considered his wife's apprehension while, at the same time, he tried to hide his own. He'd gotten the stove going pretty good and hot in the past, but only now second-guessed himself after Carla had voiced her concern.

"Mm, nah. I think it's fine."

"You *think*?"

He turned to her and smiled. "It'll be fine," he said reassuringly. "That thing's built to take a lot more than what I've put in there. We're safe."

She folded her arms across her chest and raised an eyebrow.

"Besides," Doug said, "that's what we have smoke detectors for, right?"

Her arms dropped dubiously at her sides. "Seriously, Doug?"

He laughed and threaded his hands between her waist and arms, hugging her close.

"Come on, you think I'd let the house burn down?"

Another raised eyebrow. "Well, no…not purposely."

"Oh, so just inadvertently, then?"

"Yeah, something like that." She wrinkled her nose in the way Doug has always found cute and sexy and leaned in to kiss him. Her lips are amazingly soft and full—one of the many qualities with which he'd fallen in love. As he pressed his lips against hers, it was just like the first time he'd kissed her. In fact, every time he kisses her is like the first time.

She slowly pulled away and began to walk out of the room. "I just finished reading with Janie. You gonna say goodnight?"

"Yes," he said. "I'll be there in a minute.

Doug and Carla married shortly before moving into their home. They had dated for six years before Doug finally summoned the courage to pop the question. It came as no surprise to any of their family or friends when the engagement announcements arrived in the mail. It was even less of a surprise when they set their wedding date only four months after the announcement.

Getting married, to some, is often viewed as two people beginning their life together. For Doug and Carla, their life had begun over a half-decade ago, so "being together" wasn't something with which they were unfamiliar. However, their home was brand new, so there was still an element of freshness—a *new*ness to their life.

They built their home in 2001 on top of a small, quarter-acre plot in Southwick, Massachusetts—an L-shaped ranch situated far enough away from the road that their daughter could play in the front yard, but also with enough room out back for the deck, swing set, and pick-up games of Wiffle-Ball homerun derby with the neighbor, Wayne.

Their street is safe, but a well-traveled one. It's one of the main arteries in Southwick on which school buses routinely run student pick-ups for the elementary and high schools in town. They also have their fair share of tractor-trailers and Connecticut residents passing through, as their home is only one mile north of the state line.

Familiar and foreign collided all at once when they spent their first night in the new home—a night like every other night they would experience those first few years. Nights that could only be described as uneventful with nothing so much as aberrant or deviating from the norm.

The first of many events that would soon come to define their home life occurred during the fall of 2011.

Doug turned back to the stove and gave the coals one last look. They were blazing quite brightly like a hot orange bed of embers beneath the reaching flames of a campfire. A small part of him wondered if it really *was* safe. But then another part actually felt comforted knowing that, yes, they *did* have smoke alarms in the house and, yes, they *were* there to alert in case of an emergency.

As he left the room, he wondered if his wife would still trust him if she ever heard his inner thoughts.

Outside, light from a street lamp up the road caught Doug's eye and he moved toward the large bay window in the front room. The lamp cast a soft, yellowish glow that fell over a large parked construction vehicle. Doug read the word CATERPILLAR on the side of the great machine and wondered how much longer construction of the new shopping complex would continue before it was finished. The town leaders had promised residents a quick three-month project, but then came one budget issue and two delayed proposals; though the job was already four months in, they'd barely finished clearing the land. Foundations had yet to be poured and the constant back-and-forth of the vehicles often clogged up traffic on their road. Not to mention, it was an eyesore. Temporary, yes, but still an eyesore.

When Doug reached Janie's room, she was already tucked into her bed, but the light on her nightstand was still on. Carla had left it for him to turn out after he said goodnight.

As he stood in the doorway, he watched her squeeze her eyes overly tight. He could even see her lips quivering in an effort to hold back laughter. She loved pretending to be asleep for Doug and then "surprising" him with a shriek as he approached her to say goodnight. He paused for a moment and stared at her reverently. The road to having a child hadn't been an easily paved one.

Carla hadn't wanted kids. At least that's what she'd told him early on when they began dating. And while many men would have had a problem with that, Doug, too, didn't want kids, so the two of them felt they were a perfect match. Soul mates. When he and Carla met, Doug already had one nephew whom he loved dearly, and still does. But for Doug, having a child of his own was never something he wanted or needed—one reason being that he enjoyed his freedom, the other being because his nephew hated him. Or so Doug claimed.

Carla would often tease him, saying "hate" is too strong a word: "I'm sure he doesn't *hate* you." Doug's belief was that children are very much like animals: Once they sense a level of discomfort or uncertainty in you, they likewise become uncomfortable and uncertain. The point at which they recognize this uncertainty is about the same time they realize they're much better off in the arms of a person who is *not* uncomfortable around children. So his nephew cried around him. A lot.

One afternoon, many years ago when Doug was still a teenager, he was left alone to babysit his then one-year-old nephew, Paul. Doug's brother, Luke, had been working that day, and Doug's mother and sister-in-law decided to take a walk to the convenience store down the street. So they left Doug to watch Paul for twenty minutes.

It was easily the most uncomfortable twenty minutes of Doug's young life.

He and Paul sat on his mother's couch watching TV. Paul was very quiet at first. He sat on one end of the couch, staring straight forward. Doug sat on the opposite end, only casually paying attention to the TV and not knowing what to do or say. He figured he could simply sit there in silence (as long as Paul also sat in silence), but that was no way to watch a child. There were a few toy cars and trains on the floor and on the coffee table in front of them. So, rather than sit in silence and hope for the best, Doug decided he would try to play with his nephew.

He picked up a train and moved it along the edge of the coffee table, making "choo-choo" noises as he pushed it along. Paul's stone face turned toward the train. He didn't smile, but his expression softened a bit and Doug started to think maybe this wasn't going to be so awkward. He picked up the train and "jumped" it from the coffee table to the couch. Paul's eyes followed the train the whole way. Then Doug pushed the toy train closer to Paul. Eventually, he "chugged" it up onto his tiny bare feet. Paul wiggled his toes a bit, but still his expression didn't change.

Then Doug asked him, "Hey Paul, whose train is this?" Doug smiled as big and bright as he could. "Is this Paul's train? Can Uncle Doug play with your train?"

After that, his attempt to get his nephew to like him went to hell. Paul's eyebrows arched and his flat lips formed into a small, inverted horseshoe. Then his eyelids tightened and his mouth opened to let out a howl. One minute had passed since Doug's mother and sister-in-law left and already he'd managed to make this kid cry. All he'd wanted to do was play trains with him.

It wasn't always that bad, though. Eventually, his nephew, and later on, his niece, grew to love him as much as he loved them. Doug playfully told Carla it only took until they were around two years of age before his niece and nephew warmed up to him. He wondered if it was something he had done, or if they'd simply grown accustomed to having him around, but they soon loved Doug and that made him happy.

Doug knelt down next to Janie's bed and leveled his face with hers. "Hey, Sweetie, are you awake?"

"Daddy!" she exclaimed, her eyes popping open. She rose from the bed slightly.

"Agh!" Doug pseudo-screamed. "You got me!"

She giggled as Doug reached out and tickled her sides.

"Guess what, Daddy?"

"What?"

"When I went swimming at school today, I held my breath under water for seven seconds!"

"Oh, my goodness! How did you hold your breath for that long?"

"Because I'm a good swimmer, Daddy."

One of Doug's favorite pastimes was watching Janie learn a new skill or concept. His fascination with her development grew exponentially with her intelligence. Even something as minute as her learning a new word—or rather, how to pronounce a new word—amazed him. He had thought it cute when Janie first tried to say the word "bigger," but it ended up coming out as "burger." Daddy, I wanna watch a movie on the *burger* TV!" He quickly fell madly in love with her innocence. Then, one day, she asked to watch the "bigger" TV, and a simple word became one less thing she would ever learn.

The way her mind digested new information and how she understood something she hadn't just a day before both astounded and saddened him. Even at seven she was smart for her age, and Doug could feel the tether that kept him attached to the toddler version of Janie fraying in the middle. As the years accumulated, it filled Doug with pride to see his daughter grow and mature, but a tiny piece of his heart broke off every time he saw a bit of her youth slip away. On the eventual day when Janie became a woman, Doug knew that tether would eventually break and all he'd be left with were the memories of a child and her adoring father as they grew up together.

"I think I know someone who can swim better than you," Doug said.

"Who, Daddy?"

"Nemo!"

Janie laughed. Although the movie was older than she, the story about the little orange-and-white clown fish was one of her favorites.

"Wanna read a book?" she asked.

Gotta love seven year-olds and their bedtime-stalling attempts.

"Hmm...didn't your mom already read to you?"

"Yeah, but she's not as good as you," Janie pleaded.

"I heard that!" Carla called out from down the hall. Doug and his daughter laughed. He laughed even harder when he heard that little hitch in Janie's giggle. It was kind of like a hiccup; almost a snort, but not as abrupt. And it warmed his heart every time he heard it.

"All right," he said, "I'll read ONE more book, but after that, it's time for night-night. Okay?"

She stared at him with her warm, brown eyes; her long, dark curls framing her face, just like her mother's. "Okay, Daddy."

He walked over to her bookcase and pulled out her favorite, *The Princess and the Frog*, and he sat down to read.

She was asleep before he turned the last page.

CHAPTER 2

Doug woke up hungry. He'd eaten a large dinner earlier that night, so this seemed a bit odd, but hardly a concern. He sat up in bed, careful not to wake Carla, and reached for his glasses on the nightstand. He looked at the clock on the dresser across the room. It was two in the morning. Not exactly time for a snack, but he needed something to settle the monster in his stomach and go back to sleep.

As he sat in bed trying to decide whether or not to eat something, a sound from the great room broke his thoughts. He first wondered if it was only his subconscious having interfered with his decision of whether or not to get something to eat. But then, with full attention, it happened again. This time the sound of metal-on-rock was unmistakable.

Someone had just shoveled coal into the stove.

Carla laid unconscious next to him so it had to be Janie who'd added coal to the fire. It was the only logical assumption.

When Janie was four, she'd started asking about the stove. She didn't understand what a coal stove was or what it did, but she did understand things like "ouchies" and "boo-boos," so after Doug explained to his little girl, "If you touch the coal stove, it will give you an 'ouchie,'" she got the idea. After all, the same explanation had worked with the kitchen stove; Janie had never once touched the burners or even the door, so logic suggested it would work with the coal stove as well. And to the best of Doug and Carla's knowledge, she'd never touched the coal stove.

Doug waited a bit longer and listened for either the sound of another scrape of shovel against coal, or that of his daughter's quick feet scurrying down the hall and back into her bedroom in an attempt not to be caught.

Unless Doug had misinterpreted the sound and an intruder was in the house.

In a single motion, Doug ripped away the sheets and swung his legs over the edge of the bed. He reached for the door handle and turned it slowly, careful not to open the door too loudly—the hinges were freshly greased, but the handles themselves had loosened with age. One could be standing in the great room and easily hear the door to Doug's bedroom open.

He stepped into the hall and his heart skipped a beat. The sudden fear of potentially seeing a stranger in the house caused him to pause. He waited and listened for a follow-up to what he'd heard moments ago. A thumping in his ears began to roll. When he heard nothing more, he quietly walked the four steps to Janie's room. Her door was ajar. Doug and Carla always left her door open a bit. The light above the kitchen stove cascaded down the hall and, while it certainly wasn't bright enough to keep Janie awake, provided just enough light in case she ever woke up scared or needed to use the bathroom. Tonight, however, she was asleep soundly.

Doug pushed open the door a bit further, enough to sneak into the room without allowing much more light. He stepped softly toward her bed. She didn't flinch as he moved, and made no indication she was only feigning sleep. When he reached the edge of her bed, Doug stopped and studied her seemingly unconscious appearance. Her breathing was slow, her breaths infrequent. Her mouth rested open slightly. Doug had witnessed this kind of deep sleep before and knew it was genuine. Janie hadn't been out of bed. She hadn't touched the coal shovel or the hod next to the stove. He began to wonder if he'd actually heard anything at all, or if the noise had occurred in a dream—a false sense of realism manifested by his subconscious.

No—he'd definitely been lying awake in bed. The same thoughts had torn through his head when he heard coal shoveled into the stove a second time.

My god...an intruder!

He spun around and left Janie's room as quietly as he'd entered.

As Doug walked further down the hallway and approached the kitchen, he could now see partially into the great room. The light was noticeably brighter, much more than when he'd retired to his bedroom. Perhaps Carla had woken during the night and left a light on? He knew she suffered from insomnia every so often; when she couldn't sleep, she'd often sit on the couch, turn on a lamp, and read until she got tired. But Doug was a light sleeper and almost always woke up at the slightest movement in bed.

He reached the end of the hallway and turned into the kitchen, which was long and flowed into the great room. From his position, Doug could see the great room's farthest wall. The only thing he couldn't see was the coal stove, which was tucked into the corner of the room and out of sight for the moment.

With sleep-filled eyes, the light above the kitchen stove was enough to help navigate the room, but not as luminous as what he saw in the great room. That light seemed almost animated, moving around and dancing along the walls in waves. That's when Doug made the connection: The light in the great room wasn't cast by a lamp…it had been made by the fire behind the tempered glass door of the coal stove. The flame had raged hours ago, but it surely would have abated by now…

Doug proceeded through the kitchen and toward the great room, stopping at the breakfast bar—the semi-divider of the two rooms. He was constantly aware of the possibility there still might be an intruder in the house. With no weapon at his disposal, he considered backtracking and taking a knife from the block on top of the counter, but decided against it. The last thing Doug wanted was to give the intruder, if unarmed, any opportunity to obtain a weapon.

His feet froze at the down-step—a four-inch drop from the kitchen floor.

Doug half-expected someone to leap out from behind the bar, but no such attack occurred. Yet. He breathed slowly and again considered turning around to search for some form of protection—a baseball bat, a mallet, anything—but ultimately felt such a maneuver was too risky.

As adrenaline sent hot fire through his chest and limbs, he began to welcome the attack of a stranger. It surprised Doug even then how his mind had changed from near-flight to fight. He felt *ready* for an assault. Through all his adolescent years, he'd been one of the kindest, most passive children in school. He never fought. If anything, he looked for every opportunity to avoid conflict. But now, as his pulse raged forth, and out of instinct to protect his family, he felt an unprecedented urge to quarrel with whoever was lurking in the shadows of his home. He even began to feel sorry for the person who might be waiting just around the corner, thinking they might have the element of surprise on their side.

Oh, you shall be the one surprised.

He stepped down and turned the corner.

There was nobody in the great room. Doug's bare feet landed softly on the tile surface of the foyer to no advance of another. He looked around the room and the surge of adrenaline faded as he realized there was no intruder. He watched the firelight dance along the walls and basked in the warmth of the stove.

He stared at the fire licking the glass window of the stove's door.

Impossible. I fed those coals hours ago...

And yet there they were, burning bright and hot. Standing barefoot on the tile floor at this hour would normally have sent an icy chill through his heels and up his calves, but tonight the tile was warm. The whole house was warm, but especially so in the great room.

Doug found the electric thermostat on the wall behind him and leaned close to check the temperature of the room. It read seventy-two degrees. However, when he pressed the "setting" button, it read sixty-two. The thermostat was set a full ten degrees lower than the room's current temperature.

He curiously approached the stove again. It sat on a brick platform in front of the fireplace; a pipe led from the back of the stove to the chimney. Doug pulled a flashlight from the mantle—he always kept one handy in the event of a power outage—and checked all the stove parts. Everything seemed to be working correctly. He studied the door closely. There were no cracks and no fissures in either the glass or the iron. The door also swung evenly and closed firmly.

Satisfied with his examination, he backed away and stared at the stove a bit longer. Maybe the coals somehow fell into a perfect arrangement, a configuration that allowed them to burn longer and hotter than usual? He supposed it was possible. He wasn't an expert in coal fuel; for all he knew, they might burn out in another fifteen minutes. Perhaps he was only now witnessing their end of life, much the way a dying star burns hottest and brightest just before burning its final gases. He placed the flashlight back on the mantle and made to leave.

His feet temporarily left the ground when he saw Janie standing there in her pajamas and holding her blanket.

"Daddy, I'm hot," she said.

Apparently she hadn't heard the howl of surprise from Doug's mouth and didn't see him clutch his chest as he tried to recover from the unexpected shock of her appearance. He took a few deep breaths, waited for his heart to calm and then knelt down—partly because he wanted to speak to her at her level, and partly because he was still uncertain of his legs' ability to provide balance just yet.

He rested a hand on her shoulder. She was warm to the touch, even through her pajamas. "What's the matter, J-bird? Do you feel sick?"

Doug and Carla have always been aware that "J-bird" wasn't the most appropriate nickname for a little one (unless that little one somehow found herself incarcerated at the age of seven), but given her first initial and the fact that "bird" was common informal slang for "woman" in the United Kingdom, they found it to be cute and rather innocent. Eventually, it stuck.

"No," Janie said, "I'm just hot and I can't sleep."

He pressed his palm against her forehead. It wasn't as warm as when he touched her shoulder—her forehead actually felt normal by contrast—so Doug figured it had probably just been warm and stuffy in her room.

"How about we get you a glass of water and I'll turn on your ceiling fan?" he asked.

She nodded.

Having completely forgotten the reason he'd woken up, Doug walked with her back to the kitchen. He removed a cup from the cabinet and drew some water from the Brita container in the refrigerator. When the cup was half full, he gave it to Janie.

"Here, Sweetie. Drink this and we'll go turn on your fan."

She finished her water and took his hand as they walked out of the kitchen, down the hall, and into her bedroom. Doug tucked her in with only a sheet; he left the heavy comforter rolled up at the bottom of her bed.

"If you get cold," he said, holding an edge of the comforter, "just pull this over you." She simply nodded as Doug pointed to the comforter. He moved to the door and flipped the switch to engage the ceiling fan. It started up silently, eventually moving the stagnant air enough to create a comfortable atmosphere.

"Daddy?" she asked as he stepped out the door.

"Yes?"

"Can you leave my door open?"

"Sure, Sweetie." He pushed the door wide open. "'Night, J-Bird."

"G'night."

She rolled over on her side and tucked her blanket under her arm. Doug stood at her door a few minutes longer until he heard the faintest hint of a snore. When she was asleep, he went back to bed.

In the morning, Doug was the first to wake up. He walked down the hall and into the kitchen to start the coffee maker.

When he walked by Janie's room, her door was closed completely.

CHAPTER 3

At work, Doug's thoughts were consumed by the previous night's events. The unusually flaming, extra-hot coal was an anomaly and he figured it to be nothing more than just a peculiar, one-time occurrence. But what the hell made that noise? Doug was sure someone had been up, feeding the coal stove, but nobody had been awake except him.

Did I sleepwalk? Impossible.

Doug knew he'd woken up to the sound. His mind hadn't created it.

He drove out his thoughts and tried to focus on work. A manager in the call center of a global financial institution, Doug trained his eyes on his laptop. He steered his mouse and pointed the cursor over a file called "productivity" and opened it. The file opened and he stared at a spreadsheet filled with the names of his employees. As he clicked through the various tabs in the document, he saw groups of numbers and figures—call times, hold times, first call resolutions, number of agents available. After clicking through a half dozen tabs, the numbers began to morph together as his efforts to concentrate failed him.

And why did Janie close her door? She always sleeps with her door open...

Doug knew kids grow up and out of old habits. Perhaps Janie was starting to grow out of the I-need-to-sleep-with-my-door-open phase. The increased warmth in the house certainly would have explained why Janie had woken up; after all, she'd complained of being hot. But it still bothered Doug that she had closed her door. He wondered if the light above the kitchen stove had been too bright, or maybe a draft in her room pushed the door closed.

But we don't have strong drafts in the house, definitely not strong enough to push a bedroom door closed completely...

He forced the memory from his mind again, but with help this time: the phone on his desk rang, returning his thoughts to his current task. The name that registered on the phone's display was that of a member of his company's sales force. Doug picked up the phone.

"Douglas Mitchell."

The voice on the other line immediately launched into a complaint about one of Doug's direct reports, the abrupt nature of which was only assuaged by the knowledge of this particular salesperson being a chronic complainer of small things. Doug could have fought back with a verbal tirade of his own, but it was still early in the day and he didn't have enough anger to respond in kind. He simply sat back in his chair and rolled his eyes as the caller barked out phrases like "not a team player" and "in the interest of client satisfaction…"

When the salesperson finished her lengthy vent, Doug advised he would speak to the agent in question and ensure it didn't happen in the future. Before the salesperson had a chance to respond, he replaced the receiver in the cradle.

Doug stood from his desk and surveyed the call center. The room was organized by long rows of cubicles with walls high enough to afford some privacy, but anyone of average height would have a good view of the tops of the customer service agents' heads when standing. Doug located the subject of the conversation he'd had only moments ago and proceeded to his desk. He'd already decided not to berate the poor guy, but only remind him to be mindful of whom he is talking to when *certain* sales people call. It wasn't how he preferred to start his day, but it gave him another reason to stay focused and prevent his mind from obsessing on what happened the night before.

He would begin to obsess about it when it happened again the following night.

Just as he did the night before, Doug woke up hungry and hot. He pulled an arm out from under the sheets and ran his hand across his forehead. He felt bubbles of moisture collect on his palm and fingers. To his right, Carla was once again fast asleep. Somehow, her body was immune to the increased heat in the house.

In an effort to prevent the stove from firing like it had the previous night, Doug made sure to distribute the coals evenly within the stove, so the fire would burn more consistently throughout the night. There was no way the coals would burn that hot past midnight.

He reached for his glasses on the nightstand and stared across the room at the clock. It read two-nineteen a.m.

Shunk!

It was the same sound he'd heard the night before. This time it was louder. He knew right away his mind wasn't playing any games; his subconscious had not duped him in any way. Someone had just dumped a shovelful of coal into the stove.

Shunk!

Doug peeled the sheets from his sweat-soaked body, rose quickly from the bed and plunged into the hallway. He stopped and waited as he stared down the hall. The air was completely still and he remained motionless as he stood outside the bedroom. He even slowed his breathing in order to hear anything and everything more clearly. Doug half-expected to see Janie round the corner from the kitchen on her way back to her bedroom. He had been out of the bed and into the hallway less than a second after hearing the last sound. Had Janie been out of her room, there was no way he would have missed her.

Having been asleep for hours, Doug's eyes were well-adjusted to the darkness. He stared absently at the grout-grid of the tile floor in the kitchen, following each line and making a staircase, like a 2-D version of Q-Bert. As he played this game, his eyes on the floor, he stayed still and waited for the next sound, or for Janie to appear, but neither occurred. He proceeded to follow the same journey as the one from the night before.

He walked slowly down the hall, stopping only to peer into Janie's room. She was in her bed, asleep. He didn't go into her room this time; the hunger he felt caused his stomach to bark and demanded sustenance. In the quiet of the night, he didn't want his hunger pangs to wake her up, so he kept moving.

He walked into the kitchen. This time he was less nervous than the night before. He opened the refrigerator; there wasn't much in the way of leftovers except for half an apple pie Carla had baked earlier. It wasn't Doug's usual middle-of-the-night food of choice, but he would make do.

He served himself a slice of the pie and then moved through the kitchen toward the great room. The warm, orange glow, cast by the fire from the coals and onto the walls, was alive and even brighter than the night before.

Doug shoved a bite into his mouth and stepped around the breakfast bar and down into the foyer. When he turned toward the stove, it was burning brightly.

He felt as if it were mocking him, like it were a living entity that took pleasure in his ignorance—in his not knowing how the hell it could possibly be burning so hot at such a late hour.

He was also concerned about the noise. All day at work he'd debated whether or not the sounds had been real or if he'd dreamt them. This time, he knew what he'd heard. As he took another bite of the pie, he wondered if maybe he hadn't heard the shoveling of coal, specifically, but maybe the shovel itself shifting and sliding against the brick fireplace. Maybe he'd left it unbalanced and somehow, hours later, gravity had finally pulled it into a more secure and standing position.

Bullshit. I know what a shovel sliding against brick sounds like, just as I know what it sounds like when the metal tip digs into a bucket of fresh coals.

So then what was it? What the hell could have caused or created the noise he heard?

"Daddy?"

"Shit!" he yelled. As he jumped, Doug spun around and saw Janie standing behind him. Chewed-up chunks of apple pie were on his shirt; the rest of the slice had flown from his hand and landed somewhere on the dark floor. Even with his startled outburst, Janie didn't even flinch. Her eyes were tired. Her shoulders lacked any tension and energy. She held her blanky in her hands, but there was slack in her arms and fingers. There were no signs she'd been awake for a while. It was clear the child had just woken up within the last minute or two.

Doug leaned against the edge of the breakfast bar, steadying himself. "Sorry, Sweetie..." he said, nearly out of breath. "Daddy didn't... know you were... there."

"I'm hot," she said.

What? No apology for almost knocking Daddy on his ass for the second night in a row? No? Eh, oh well. You're only seven. I'll give you a pass.

The initial shock having passed, Doug slowed his breathing once again, enough to put together more than two words. "Do you want to sleep without the comforter again? Will that help?"

She nodded.

"Okay, let's go back to your room."

When they got back to her room, he paused at the door and once again turned on the fan. Janie kept walking and crawled into her bed. After turning on the fan, Doug walked over to the bed. In doing so, he managed to trip over an object in the middle of the floor. Then another.

And another.

"Daddy," she said softly, her voice still weakened by sleep. "Be careful. Those are my dolls."

He looked down. It was so dark in her room he hadn't seen them.

"Sorry, J-Bird." He bent down to pick one up. "Want me to put one in bed with you?"

"NO!" she hissed and leaned up on one elbow. "No," she said again, softer this time.

"Okay. Sorry, Janie." He placed the doll back on the floor. When he did, he noticed there were more than two dolls. There were close to a dozen, arranged in a semi-circle next to her bed.

Before he could ask, Janie already had an answer ready: "They have to stay there. They're watching."

Doug was surprised by this new development. Janie had played with dolls ever since she was two years old, but she'd never set her dolls on *watch* before.

Doug curbed a smile. "What are they watching, Sweetie?" he asked.

Janie hesitated. Doug felt like maybe there was something she wanted to tell him, but she wasn't going to divulge it easily. Maybe if he pressed a little harder…

But it was late. Far too late to get into a conversation with a seven-year-old regarding the seating arrangement of dolls.

"They're just watching," she offered casually, as if no further explanation was needed. "And they have to stay there tonight."

Doug had to work even harder to stifle a laugh at the matter-of-fact tone of her voice.

"Okay, Janie, I won't move them. Sleep good."

He leaned down and kissed her head.

"G'night, Daddy."

"Night, sweetheart."

CHAPTER 4

In the morning, Doug woke up in an empty bed. A fine mist of sunlight sprayed in through the window, clinging to the air in the room like a soft, yellow fog. On the dresser, the clock read eight twenty-three a.m. A smile curled his lips — Doug could count on one hand the number of times he'd slept past seven since Janie was born and he silently thanked Carla for letting him sleep in.

Carla sat at the kitchen table reading the morning paper and eating breakfast. It was Saturday. She was reading the weekend edition of the Springfield paper, which served most towns in western Massachusetts. Doug's movement in the hallway caught her attention and she turned to see him emerging from the bedroom.

"Hey, sleepyhead," she said. Her long, dark hair was in disarray, tousled on top of her head and in front of her blue eyes.

"I'm sorry, I don't know why I slept so late," Doug said as he stretched his arms above his head.

"It's okay," she said as she stood up from the table. "I know you were up last night with Janie so I thought I'd let you sleep in."

Doug moved closer to her, put his arms around her waist, and kissed her. "Thank you." He looked around. He heard the TV in the other room, but not any sign of Janie. By now she'd usually be talking to herself, staging a dialogue between at least two dolls.

He motioned toward the great room. "Janie in there?"

Carla nodded. "She's watching TV."

"Cool," he said as he moved through the kitchen.

"She seems a bit off, though," she said.

"Off?"

"Yeah. Not sure if she's grumpy because she didn't sleep well or if she's coming down with something."

"Hmm," Doug pondered. "Did you check her forehead? She feel warmer than usual?"

She shrugged her shoulders. "Not really, no."

"Okay. Probably nothing, then."

He walked toward the great room, allowed his hand to glide along the smoke-green, laminate surface of the breakfast bar, and found Janie sitting quietly on the floor watching cartoons. She didn't acknowledge his presence and only stared blankly at the TV.

"Hey, J-Bird, can I get a morning hug?"

Janie slowly rose to her feet, as if it hurt to stand. She turned and moved toward her father. Her head and shoulders slumped forward and she dragged her feet as she walked.

"Aww, are you upset that Daddy woke you up last night?" he asked, trying to encourage a smile out of her. But as she reached Doug's outstretched arms, she didn't hug him but merely leaned into him, letting her arms rest limp at her sides. Doug held her, pressed his cheek to her forehead to feel if she was warm.

"You feeling okay, J-Bird?" he asked.

Janie tilted her head to look up at him. Her eyelids fell halfway down, nearly closed. "I don't feel like watching TV anymore," she said. Her voice sounded tired. "Can I go back to sleep in my room?"

He was concerned, but only slightly. After all, he'd slept past eight o'clock. Surely, if he was tired enough to sleep that long, then it would make sense that she was also tired. "Sure, Sweetie, go ahead."

Janie pulled away from Doug's arms and walked, head down, her shoulders rolled forward, through the kitchen and toward the hallway. Doug tried once more to solicit a more enthusiastic response.

"When you get up, I'll make your favorite breakfast: waffles!"

She didn't even turn around. "That's okay, you don't have to," she said weakly.

Janie loves waffles, he thought. *She probably just needs some rest.*

Janie continued walking until she reached her bedroom and closed the door behind her.

"What do you think that's all about?" he asked Carla.

"Not sure," she said. "I left my *Understanding Seven-Year-Olds* manual in the car."

Doug smirked. "Nice."

He sat on a stool in front of the breakfast bar and rubbed his eyes again. Sleep was only slowly fading from his brain and he badly needed caffeine. When he pulled his hands away, he found himself staring down into a fresh, steaming cup of light-brown coffee.

"Well, aren't you an angel," he said.

"You're lucky I love you," Carla quipped. "Especially since you've been blasting the heat in this place lately. I was sweating last night."

He still hadn't told her about the stove.

"Yeah, about that," he began, "I woke up to some really strange sounds the last couple nights."

"Booooo..." Carla said, raising her hands and wiggling her fingers. The only thing missing that would have completed the ghost pantomime was a white sheet.

"No, seriously."

"Yeah?" She dropped the Halloween act and folded her arms over her chest. "What kinds of sounds?"

Doug filled her in on the past two nights, including everything from the sound of the coal being shoveled into the stove, to him waking up hungry, to Janie's behavior.

"Wow," Carla said. "So I guess she really is just tired." For a moment, it was as if she'd entirely dismissed everything else he told her.

"Riiight," he started. "So, nothing to say about the rest?"

"What? Oh, right. I meant to tell you: We have spirits in the house, honey!" She spread her arms in a very magician-like *ta-da!* motion.

"I wasn't aware I married a comedienne," Doug said.

She dropped her arms. "Well, come on, you tell me you hear spooky noises at night, the furnace—"

"Stove," he interjected.

"—is allegedly channeling the fires of hell, and Janie's playing with her dolls in the middle of the night. What do you want me to say? 'Honey, let's get an exorcist in here?'"

"Whoa, whoa! Nobody's talking about anyone getting exorcised. I just think it's weird, that's all."

She stared at him dubiously. "I think you watch too many of those ghost hunting shows."

Doug laughed. "Oh, stop."

"Hey," Carla insisted, "some people love having spirits in their home." Her eyes went suddenly wide. "Wait a minute! What if we *do* have spirits?"

Doug could tell she was now mocking him.

"That could be fun!" she continued. "We could ask them about stuff…like how come it takes three hours for Doug to change the oil in his car?"

Doug laughed even harder.

Carla continued, "Or, how come when Doug goes out to mow the lawn, he ends up drinking beer with Wayne and talking about sports until the sun goes down?"

"Are you finished having fun?" Doug asked, the smile having not yet left his mouth.

Carla stared back at him with persistent eyes.

"I get it," he said. "I was just looking for a little honest opinion."

She walked closer, rested her elbows on top of the breakfast bar, and leaned against her folded hands. "Okay. You want honesty?"

Doug nodded.

"I think you're stressed," she said flatly.

Doug straightened in his chair. His eyes narrowed. "Stressed? How? With work?"

"Well, think about it," Carla said. "How many conferences have you done this year? Four? Five? You usually do one per year at best."

"Yeah, but—"

"And how many side jobs have you helped your brother with this year?"

"Well, he's—"

"And think of all Janie's extracurricular stuff: soccer, floor hockey…"

"All right," Doug finally cut her off. "I know…it's been a busy year."

"And the holidays are right around the corner."

"I'm doing my best. The company only sends its best and brightest to conferences, so it's a compliment to me that they want me out so much. If I tell them 'no' and I just stop going, I won't be helping my career or this family."

As a senior employee at his company, Doug was often relied upon to represent his firm at various customer service summits around the United States. In the beginning, he only attended one event per year. But, as clients and other customer service organizations got to know him—and like him—Doug's manager urged him to attend more events, claiming his "wonderful personality," "calming demeanor," and "anything-for-the-client attitude" brought much positive visibility for their company. After nearly nine years with the company, Doug was averaging one event almost every two months.

Carla rested her hands in his. "I know, Hon, and I'm not telling you how or when or in what capacity to do your job. I'm just asking you to think about what's going on and what might be causing it." She let the alternative hang in the air for a few seconds before saying it: "Besides ghosts."

He sighed. She had a point and he knew it. It was one of the reasons he married her. Not only was she blessed with model-like looks, she was smart as hell.

"I know," he said. He swallowed his pride and stared into her eyes. "Next time there's an offer to go to a conference, I'll make something up and tell them I can't go. That should buy me another four or five months, maybe."

"I think that's a wonderful choice," she said.

He smiled and she smiled back at him. Then he rose from the stool. "I'm starving. You want something?" he asked as he walked into the kitchen.

"I'm just going to have some cereal."

"Sounds good," he said as he reached for an overhead cabinet. When he pulled the round handle, the cabinet door swung open, seemingly by itself, and the plastic cereal-saver fell out and onto the counter. The lid popped off and Cheerios spilled onto the floor.

"What the hell?" he said. "Did you see that?"

"Hon," Carla put her hands on her hips. "How'd you do that?" Her tone was only slightly accusatory.

"I didn't," he said defensively. "It's like it just jumped out at me." He stared back and forth from the spilled cereal on the counter, then to the floor, then into the open cabinet at the box of crackers on which the cereal had been precariously sitting. Then he turned to her. "When's the last time you took the cereal out?"

Her eyes flicked up at the ceiling as she thought about it. "Probably yesterday. Why?"

"Did you happen to notice it was sitting on top of an unstable box of crackers?"

She tilted her head. "Really? You're gonna blame me?"

"Daddy, I know who pushed the cereal out."

Doug was surprised to hear Janie's voice. He was even more surprised by the lightness of her tone, given the latency with which she spoke a few minutes ago. Doug turned around. Strangely, Janie appeared fully awake and alert. She stood plainly, her shoulders and back straight and didn't slouch. Her eyes weren't tired either.

What the hell?

"Feeling better?" he asked.

"Yup."

No further explanation.

With no excuse or desire to further explore Janie's sudden change in mood, Doug let it go. "Well, do you wanna help me clean this up so we can have breakfast?"

"Sure."

She dropped down to her knees and scooped the cereal into cupped hands until she couldn't hold any more.

Doug pulled out a used plastic grocery bag from a closet and held it open as Janie emptied her hands into it.

"Tell you what," he said. "I'll take care of the rest. Why don't you go sit at the table and mommy will pour you a bowl."

"Okay."

He shot Janie a wink. "And tell whoever knocked over the cereal that we like it to stay *in* the box before we eat it."

Janie either didn't catch his sarcasm or didn't care when she said, "I already told him."

Doug paused a moment, cut a quick glance at Carla who mouthed the words, *I have no idea*. He turned back to Janie and, with a tone somewhere between curious and patronizing, asked, "Who was it, J-Bird?"

"It was the man who was playing with my dolls last night."

CHAPTER 5

Long before Janie was born, Carla and Doug assumed they would simply get married and never have kids and be completely happy. They figured to be the envy of all married couples *with* children—the couple who gets to travel and see the world and never have to answer to anybody but themselves. They could get away for a long weekend without having to worry about how many diapers they'd need to bring, or how many sippy-cups they would need, or if the pack-and-play would fit in the room where they were staying. Their lives would be perfect.

Then the alarm on Carla's biological clock went off.

They were lying in bed one Saturday afternoon after Carla and Doug had just made love—a "nooner." She had been running her fingers through Doug's hair, and he was so relaxed he had almost fallen asleep. Then she asked:

"Do you ever think about having kids?"

That was when Doug knew his life would be different. Carla needn't have spoken another word because he knew right then where the conversation was going—along with the next twenty years. Of course, it would be selfish of

Doug to claim the decision to have a child was completely Carla's; he *did* think about having kids. Often.

It was shortly after his twenty-ninth birthday when Doug really began to have thoughts:

Okay, I don't want a kid now, but what about when I'm fifty? Will I want one then? What about when I'm sixty? Will I wish I'd had a child by then?

And so he started to think about how old he would be *if* and *when* this child graduated high school. He didn't want to be too high up in his years. He didn't want to be sixty or seventy years old and watching his kid walk onto some brightly lit stage, wearing a cap and gown, shaking somebody's hand—someone who would likely be younger than Doug—accepting his or her high school diploma. So, after much discussion, he and Carla decided to try and have a child. If Carla got pregnant quickly, that meant he'd only be in his late forties when his kid graduated high school. That wasn't bad at all.

As long as I stay fit and take care of myself, I'll still be able to throw the ball around with him/her, play some catch, go canoeing—basically do all the normal stuff that dads typically do with their kids.

He was ready.

They didn't have to try very long before Doug's seed took root, and forty weeks later, Jane Reese Mitchell was born. Doug stayed in the delivery room, held Carla's hand as she gave birth and together they welcomed their daughter into the world.

She was the most beautiful thing he had ever seen.

As the doctor tended to Carla, Doug stood off to the side and watched Janie as she was handled and cleaned by the nurses. New-father thoughts filled his head:

Oh my god...that's my daughter...she's really here!

He wondered when they would let him hold her, but he never spoke up. He remained quiet, patient. When Janie was ready, he knew he would hold her.

An eternity later—only a minute or two in reality, and after the nurses had cleaned her up and swaddled her in a white-, red-, and blue-striped blanket—one of the nurses walked over and handed Janie to him. He instinctively cradled her in the nook of his left arm and softly placed his right hand over her body. Janie's eyes barely opened at first, but when they did, they looked into his and that hardened, calloused muscle that pumped under his ribs softened and melted.

Never before had he held something so helpless and so dependent on his care. He'd held his brothers' kids when they were younger, but never like this. Not when they were only five minutes old. This was different. This was special. It was a moment every parent cherishes because you only get to hold your child for the first time once.

Doug unfolded the blanket a little and reached for one of her hands. She'd been born with long fingers, much longer than he'd expected a newborn to have, and he immediately began to think she might play the guitar or piano one day. Maybe she'd be a swimmer, or play girls' lacrosse or softball.

He pressed his little finger against her hand and cried when she reflexively squeezed back. It was the first of what would be many firsts he would experience as a father: first crawl, first walk, first run. And then much, *much* later, first time driving, first date, first kiss—yikes!

The "first" that Doug never expected came when Janie told him and Carla about the other man living in their home.

Doug and Carla lay in bed that night, both trying to sleep, but unable to expel from their heads the words Janie had spoken earlier that morning. Doug had almost dismissed the comment completely, but played along, instead: "Well, we'll just ask the man not to do that again."

It sufficed in that Janie hadn't said another word about the "man," but it left Doug unable to relax for most of the day. His tension grew even worse now that it was late, and all he could think about was what time this mystery man would decide the stove was running out of coal again.

"Stop thinking about it," Carla said, as if reading his mind.

"You telling me, or yourself?" he volleyed back.

She rolled on her side and faced him. "You know kids have imaginary friends, right?"

"So you think she made it up?"

"Of course she made it up. When I was a girl, I had 'friends,'", she said, making quotations with her fingers. "They would play with me and my dollies. My mother would even tell me, 'Go play with your friends while mommy watches her soaps.'"

"She didn't!" he laughed.

"Oh, she did. Obviously it was her way of finding a little quiet, kid-free time. But it also helped me to grow out of the imaginary friend thing. I eventually got bored of my imaginary friend because I wanted to play with real people, real kids. When I stopped talking about my 'friend,' my mom could no longer use it as an excuse to watch her daytime shows. Then she started paying more attention to me."

Doug crunched his eyebrows. "So...you're telling me I should tell her to play with this 'friend' more so she grows out of it?"

Carla rolled her eyes. "No, I'm just saying it's a phase. She'll grow out of it on her own. Just stop reading more into it than what it really is. If we continue to pay attention to it, it's just going to prolong the whole thing."

Doug considered this rationale. His oldest nephew also had an imaginary friend for a while. Doug's brother would joke about it all the time, saying things like, "Paul is having a play-date with the Invisible Man...Paul rode the bus with this 'special friend' today..." Doug didn't want that for Janie, though. He didn't want her to have to endure the humility of having an imaginary friend, to be looked at as different or weird by the other kids in school or by members of his family. Deep down, though, he knew it was because *he* didn't want to look at her in that way.

"You're right," he said reluctantly. "It's probably nothing."

"There you go," she said. "Now you'll get some sleep tonight."

Doug laughed. "I wouldn't bet on it."

Carla slipped out of her t-shirt revealing her two perfectly shaped breasts. Her lips curled up on one side of her face. "What if I did something to take your mind off it?"

For the next thirty minutes, Doug forgot what they had been talking about.

***

BEEP! BEEP! BEEP!

The alarm clock on the dresser buzzed loudly, ripping Doug from his sleep. In the half-second between unconscious and awake, Doug wasn't sure if he'd fallen asleep yet, or if it was time to get up for work. His body jerked in bed as sleep was yanked away from him and the sudden jolt of adrenaline kick-started his conscious mind.

"What the f—" he began.

Carla was awake, too. She looked at him with one eye half open. "Did you set the alarm for now?"

Doug was already out of the sheets and stepping out of bed. "No, I didn't." He hurried to the dresser, reached behind the small alarm clock, and found the OFF button. The alarm went silent.

"Jesus," Carla said. "Why was it so loud?"

"I have no idea," Doug said as he lay back down. He pulled the comforter up to his chin. "It's off though, so…g'night."

Ten minutes later, the alarm went off again.

"The hell?" Doug burst out, having nearly fallen back to sleep. Carla, too, turned over.

"Shh!" she warned. "You're going to wake up Janie."

Doug ripped the sheets away and stepped down hard on the carpet. In two steps he was at the dresser. He grabbed the alarm clock and turned it in his hands. "What's with this piece of shit?"

"You probably just hit snooze, Hon."

He glared at her in the dark, but she couldn't see his dubious expression. "Yeah, that must be it," he said, his words slathered with sarcasm. "Because I've never used a goddamn alarm clock in my entire natural life."

Carla held out a hand. "Give it to me." Doug hesitated. "Come on, let me see it."

He reluctantly handed her the clock and she studied it in the dark. She cupped her hand around the front; the illuminated numbers glowed in her palm and the ruddy light spread to the back of the device.

"Ah, see that?" she said. "The Snooze is right next to the Off switch. Like I said, you probably just hit that by mistake." She pressed the button and it *clicked* with an air of finality "There, all set."

She placed the small clock back on the dresser, then walked around the bed and lay on her side, facing away from him.

"You're welcome," she said with smug pleasure.

Doug mumbled something under his breath and lay down on his back. He was bitter she'd figured it out, but he tried to let it go in the interest of getting back to sleep.

He stared at the ceiling until his eyes became heavy and his thoughts drifted off to a place that seemed real—a place he knew he'd never been before...

There were lots of trees. A forest. And there were tents spread out beneath the green canopy of leaves, branches, and above that, sky. Doug was camping with his friends. None of the ladies were around—just the guys. He remembered the last time he'd been camping; a place called the Silver Lake Hut. It had been on a mountain surrounded by the peaks of many other mountains. There was a lake nearby that gave the appearance of a silvery, mirror-like surface when the sun was directly overhead. Doug could see the lake now. He saw a beautiful woman emerge from the lake. It was Carla. She pointed at him, and then gestured seductively with her finger to come to her. Suddenly, Doug was back in the woods with the guys. His best friend shoved his face in front of Doug's. He began to make a very strange and irritating sound, like the end of a period of hockey...

BEEP! BEEP! BEEP!

"Are you *kidding* me?" he yelled.

"Daddy! Mommy!"

Doug and Carla leapt from the bed, ignoring the alarm clock. Janie yelled again as her parents were just outside her bedroom door. Doug pushed it open and flipped the switch on the wall. He squinted as the light came on and stabbed at his dilated pupils. He noticed a small area of carpet next to Janie's bed had been soiled with vomit.

"I don't feel good," Janie cried.

"Oh, baby, Mommy's here." Carla hurried to Janie's bed and cradled her in her arms.

"I'm going to get something to clean this up," Doug said and left the room. A minute later, he returned with a damp towel and a bucket. "Just in case," he said, handing the bucket to Carla. He knelt down and began to clean the vomit. Luckily, there wasn't much.

"Does your tummy hurt?" Carla asked. Janie nodded. "Do you want a little ginger ale?"

"Yes, please."

Carla flicked a quick glance at Doug. He placed the towel on the floor, stood up, and left the room.

In the kitchen, he looked toward the great room and saw light from the coal stove swelling brightly along the walls like the waves of an angry sea.

Again?

Although by now, he'd expected it.

As he pulled the door to the fridge, the bottle of ginger ale tumbled out toward him, somewhat forcefully. The bottle punched his knee and fell top-down on the floor; the cap cracked open and its contents sprayed out onto the lower cabinets and tile.

"Shit!"

"Doug?" Carla called from Janie's room. "What's going on?"

"The damn soda bottle exploded," he said as he carried the discharging bottle to the sink. He then pulled a dry towel from the linen closet across from the fridge and began cleaning the floor.

Carla and Janie now stood at the edge of the tile floor between the kitchen and the hallway. "What happened?" Carla asked.

"I have no idea," Doug said, his voice becoming frustrated. "I opened the door and the bottle came flying out at me." He stared at Carla; his eyes were two rifles, cocked and loaded with bullets of accusation. "Are you just not putting shit away correctly anymore?" He immediately heard the gravelly timbre in his voice and wished he could reclaim the words.

"Douglas!" She quickly threw a glance down at Janie and then returned his stare, held his eyes, and dared him to shoot again.

He sighed. "I'm sorry." He reached out his hand and rested it on Janie's shoulder. "I'm sorry, J-Bird."

He saw fear in her eyes and his heart tore open, bleeding cold regret into his stomach. It wasn't like him to lose his temper in front of her. Janie rarely saw her father get angry.

"You want some water instead?" he asked.

After a few tentative seconds, she murmured, "Okay."

Doug pulled a plastic cup from the cabinet above the sink and drew some water from the Brita container in the fridge. He handed it to her. Even in the dim light of the kitchen Janie already looked better. Her face had been ashen and damp when they first entered her room, but now her color came back as she slowly drank.

"How does she feel?" Doug asked.

"She was a little warm when I was holding her, but now..." Carla palmed Janie's forehead. "She feels fine."

Doug rested his hands on his hips, still frustrated, but more confused. "You feel okay to go back to bed?" he asked Janie.

"Yes."

He looked at Carla and shrugged his shoulders. "All right, well...why don't you head back to your room and I'll be there in a minute to clean up. Okay?"

"Okay," Janie said. Her voice was no longer weak, but surprisingly light. Doug thought he even heard a general pleasantness in her tone.

As she walked back to her room with the cup in her hands, she said, "Mr. Achak doesn't like ginger ale—he only drinks water."

CHAPTER 6

"Who the hell is Mr. 'Ahh-Shack?'" Doug asked.

"It's just a phase," Carla said, only slightly exasperated and in a monotone voice. "She will grow out of it."

The winter sun hid behind a veil of morning clouds. The bus had already come and picked up Janie for school, and since Doug wasn't ready to approach the subject with her yet, he hadn't bothered to ask her about her new friend's name. Moreover, neither he nor Carla had conferred about the introduction of a name to this imaginary friend until now.

Doug's cheeks, nose, and eyes all pinched together and he wiggled his shoulders as if a spider had crawled down the middle of his back. "Yeah, but it's weird, isn't it?" He casually sipped his coffee while Carla frantically tried to pick up the kitchen and great room.

"Just go to work," she sighed. "Janie's going to be fine."

Carla ran a daycare in their home. She'd worked for a childcare facility in town for several years, but after a spirited argument with her superior (and two co-workers), she decided to open a daycare in their home. In the beginning it was a challenge trying to incentivize new parents to sign up with a relatively unknown daycare, but Carla had obtained many references from parents whose children she'd cared for over the years at the town childcare center. Those parents then went on to tell *their* friends, *those* friends told *their* friends, and so on. Through mostly word of mouth, and a few homemade advertisements posted around town, her business now flourished. She had six kids—the state maximum for a single caregiver—each year.

"All right," Doug said, unnoticing of Carla's manic routine. "But what about tonight?"

Carla stopped, took a deep breath, and straightened her arms down at her sides. She then gave Doug a playful shove toward the door. "Would you just go? The kids will be here any minute, and after that I won't have any time to think. I need this place to be spotless!"

"You're right, sorry."

Doug leaned in and kissed her. He grabbed his backpack from one of the chairs that sat around the breakfast bar and carried his coffee cup to the kitchen sink.

"No meetings today," he said as he walked toward the front door. "Give me a call if you get bored."

"Ha! Try spending eight hours with a bunch of two-year-olds and tell me if you have any time to be bored!"

He smirked and walked out the door.

***

In the weeks that passed, the holidays came and went. The activity in the house grew worse. The happenings with the coal stove had decreased to the point of nonexistence; however, incidents began to occur elsewhere. Carla was the first to notice a pattern when Janie complained several times about her homework going missing.

At first, Carla had assumed it to be an honest mistake. Janie was a fantastic student. She'd never missed turning in her homework and was always forthcoming with Doug and Carla about when she had completed an assignment. Their rule about TV was that Janie had to finish all her homework at night before she could watch any shows. Twice Carla had helped Janie redo her homework in the morning as the daycare kids were showing up. Doug had stayed, too, as he had to bring Janie to school after the bus had come and gone. However, after hearing this complaint for the third morning in a row, Carla had heard enough.

She started to ask for Janie's assignments immediately after completion. Carla would then force Janie to wait in her room while she safely stored the assignment somewhere in the house, beyond Janie's reach. In the morning, when Carla would go to collect Janie's homework, it would be gone. Carla had accused Janie of spying on her as she found different places to hide the homework. Janie claimed innocence every time, but Carla was never convinced.

One night, after Carla had reached her limit as to how many times she could listen to Janie's excuses, she sent Janie to her room. She could only come out if she promised to tell Carla how she had been finding the concealed homework. Otherwise, Janie would not be allowed to eat dinner, and she'd have to spend the rest of the night alone in her room. Unable to provide what Carla deemed a plausible explanation, Janie never came out of her room until the following morning.

After that, things got even worse.

"You think this is funny?" Carla asked. She knelt on the floor of the great room, quickly snapping DVDs back into their respective cases and filing them away in the drawers of the TV stand.

"No!" Janie protested. She stood by the breakfast bar, dug through her backpack, looked inside folders and between pages of books. "I put it in here last night!"

"This needs to stop!" Carla turned and looked into the kitchen upon seeing movement in her periphery. "Doug?"

Doug had just entered the kitchen from the hallway. He wore his heavy winter coat, laptop backpack over his shoulders, and walked fast.

"Are you serious?" he asked. "Again?"

"I can't do this. I can't keep doing this," Carla repeated. "What am I supposed to tell these parents as they're dropping off their kids and I'm helping my own with her homework?" She glared again at Janie. "What am I supposed to tell them?"

"Okay, okay," Doug said. "Let's relax." He stopped in front of Janie and eyed his daughter. "J-Bird," he began calmly, "what's going on? Is everything okay at school?"

Janie started to cry. "I don't know!" she said between sobs. "I swear, I finished it! It was right here!" She held up her unzipped backpack. "I put it in here last night!"

"Are you sure?" Doug asked. He maintained a calm tone. "Do you remember doing it, or did you forget?"

"I didn't forget! I did it, I swear!"

The sound of a car door being shut outside upped the tension. Carla threw her hands up in annoyance and abruptly stood from the floor. "I don't believe this," she barked. She pointed a finger at Doug. "You're dealing with this today. I'm done. I'm absolutely done." She paced around the room, nervously straightened her hair, and smoothed the front of her shirt.

Doug patted Janie's head and walked over to Carla. He put up a hand—a peace-keeping gesture. Carla stopped pacing and took several deep breaths.

"You look fine," Doug said quietly. He then kissed her forehead. "Get to work. I've got this."

Carla only glared back at him and nodded.

"Let's go, kiddo," he said without looking back at Janie.

As Doug drove toward the school, Janie raced to complete her homework in the backseat of his Subaru Outback. Bats and balls rattled around the cargo area at every harried turn—Doug was a member of his company's co-ed softball team during the spring and summer months. His equipment hardly ever moved out of the back of his car, lest a game break out on the street.

Doug looked at Janie in the rearview mirror. "How's it coming, J-Bird? Almost done?"

Her eyes were still red and puffy, but the tear streaks had faded away. Doug was hopeful all indication she had been crying would be gone by the time he dropped her off.

"Yeah," she said. She sniffled. Her emotions were still running high, but she was doing a great job of holding them back. "Only two more problems."

"Okay. Do you think you'll be able to finish them in class? Because Daddy's really late for work."

There was a pause while Janie read the last two questions of her assignment. Then she said, "Yup, these are easy ones. They'll only take five minutes."

During the ten-minute ride to the school, Doug fought the urge to ask Janie why her homework kept going missing. He wanted to believe it was simply an innocent mistake, but he couldn't bring himself to accept that Janie had been skipping her assignments. On the other hand, he knew Carla had been verifying and then hiding them, so he was certain Janie was completing them.

Then there was the *other* alternative. Doug had been forcibly ignoring this possibility for weeks.

He looked into the mirror again. Janie was head-down, feverishly trying to finish the last two pieces of her assignment as he pulled up to the school.

"Janie?"

She looked up quickly. "Yes?"

He stared into her eyes as she wiggled a pencil between two fingers, impatiently waiting for him to speak. There was an inherent honesty in her eyes and his stomach felt hollow and guilt-ridden for even thinking of asking.

"Who keeps taking your homework?"

In that moment, Janie's once innocent eyes tightened and her head dropped like a child who'd just been tattled on. Doug saw her try to pull the curtain back in front of the wizard, but it was too late.

"I don't know."

You're lying.

"Are you sure? Because if it's not me, and it's not Mommy, who could it be? You don't see where she hides it, right?"

No response. At least, not a verbal one. But the lack of any change in expression or demeanor was in fact all the response Doug needed to confirm his suspicion. Janie remained completely still and was clearly uncomfortable having this conversation.

Doug then asked the question he'd been fearful of asking her for weeks.

"Is Mr. Achak taking your homework?"

Janie's eyes widened, but only slightly. At just seven years of age, she was damn good at keeping a secret, but not good enough. Doug had his answer. A tingle of fear crawled down his back.

Janie finally broke Doug's stare and looked out the window. "I have to go. I'm late for school, Daddy." She piled everything into her backpack, unlatched her seat belt, and got out of the car.

"Oh, okay, J-Bird. I'll see you—"

The door cut him off, slamming shut behind Janie as she hurried out of the car and into the school.

CHAPTER 7

Doug nervously approached the classroom. The last parent had emerged only moments ago and as she passed him, she offered Doug a courtesy smile and continued walking. Doug didn't recognize her. She didn't recognize him. Further, he was unable to get a read on what kind of teacher Linda Trout was based on the non-committal expression on the passing mother's face.

It was parent-teacher night and only Doug would be attending; he and Carla could not find a babysitter. Neither Doug nor Carla had ever met Janie's second-grade teacher, and while Carla usually attended these things, Doug thought she had already endured enough stress and went in her stead. Ironically, and as strained as the Carla-Janie relationship had been in recent weeks, he felt Carla was better off not attending the meeting.

He felt awkward immediately upon entering the classroom. His discomfort was only exacerbated by Ms. Trout's surprised greeting of, "Oh, hello." She had been expecting another mother. He wondered if many dads did this kind of thing.

Doug squeezed into a student's desk. He felt it strange that the teacher didn't offer a more appropriate chair—an adult chair. His eyes scanned the room and he quickly identified many objects he recognized from his elementary school days: book shelves, coat closet, half-erased items that had been written in chalk on the blackboard.

Doug fidgeted in the desk as they talked. Ms. Trout was young, even younger than Doug; he guessed her to be only three or four years removed from college. Her skin was soft and youthful, but kept the tone of a single woman who still had time for the gym six days a week. Her dark blue sport coat was professional and appropriate, and Doug couldn't help but think it was an overdone effort to look older and more refined. She also seemed uncomfortable, stuttering several times when she spoke. Likewise, her unease made Doug equally uncomfortable and he began to watch the second hand tick by on the clock above the chalkboard. It didn't help any more that Ms. Trout had been incredibly forthright about Janie's behavior.

"She's withdrawn," she said, sitting behind the desk in her classroom.

"She's what?" Doug asked. He was taken aback by how easily and effortlessly she had said it. It was as if her prior nervousness had been due to withholding this information until now. Everything Doug knew about his daughter refuted what Ms. Trout said, but he remained silent.

She continued. "At the beginning of the school year she was attentive, energetic, polite—"

"Whoa, whoa," Doug said and held up a hand. "She's impolite? Are you saying she's rude?"

"Please let me finish, Mr. Mitchell."

Doug sat back in the chair. He tried to rest his hands on top of the desk but the fingers on his left hand tapped quickly against the surface. It was a tic that always happened whenever he was nervous or angry.

"She showed me all those things at the beginning of the year," Ms. Trout continued, "and I believe she still is that sweet, smart little girl. But lately..." She hesitated, looked away from Doug and across the room as if searching for the right words among the desks, cabinets, and bookshelves, out the window, on the playground.

"Yes?" Doug prompted.

"She's somewhere else," she sighed. "It's as if, at some point during the year, and recently, she's transformed."

Doug's face twisted. "What does that mean?"

Ms. Trout spread her hands on the desk. "I know this is difficult to hear. And believe me, this is not a conversation I enjoy having."

Doug remained silent and only cued the teacher with his eyes. His fingers pounded away on the desk and his heel began to tap the floor.

"She stares out the window during class," Ms. Trout said. "She makes rude comments at awkward times, saying homework is 'stupid,' and that if the kids can do the work in class then they shouldn't have to do it at home."

Doug had a feeling he knew the reason for that particular comment.

"Overall, she seems less interested in school." She flicked a glance over toward the far wall in the room. Doug's eyes followed. There was a sink and an assortment of paint brushes drying on brown paper towels. "She got into a fight with a student over who got to use which paint color."

Doug stared at her. "Okay, now that does *not* sound like Janie."

"This particular incident just happened yesterday."

He opened his mouth to speak and then stopped. His eyes slowly fell to the floor, dragging down his head, then his shoulders, until he sat completely hunched over. He rested his forehead against his palms.

Linda Trout bit her lower lip before she said, "I know this probably isn't what you want to hear, but I think Janie would benefit from some educational assistance."

Doug looked up. All tapping of hands and feet stopped. "You mean like special needs?"

"Please understand, I'm not a doctor, Mr. Mitchell, but...in all my years of teaching, cases like this tend to do well with additional support."

"'All your years?'" he scoffed. "What are you, twenty years old?"

"Mr. Mitchell—"

"'Cases like this?' My daughter's not a *case*!" He was now standing.

"I'm sorry, Mr. Mitchell. Perhaps my language was inappropriate. What I meant was—"

"You're damn right it's inappropriate!"

"I understand you're upset, Mr. Mitchell. Perhaps you should speak to your wife about this."

"Speak to my wife? About what? About how our daughter is a little too intelligent for your inexperienced level of second-grade teaching?"

Linda Trout never deviated from her light, monotone delivery, but Doug saw the muscles in her jaw clench and unclench and knew he'd offended her. He inhaled deeply and tried to empty his frustration in one long breath. He even tried to empty his embarrassment, but knew it to be impossible.

"I'm sorry," he said.

Linda Trout's eyes didn't meet his when she said, "I think that's all for tonight, Mr. Mitchell. If you or your wife have any questions, feel free to call or email me."

Doug hesitated, not wanting to end the conversation this way. After all, she was Janie's teacher and Doug knew he should value her opinion. But when he thought of the things he could say that might prolong the discussion, he knew she might end up saying something else he didn't want to hear. Ultimately, he decided it was time to go. Doug walked out of the classroom, his head held lower than when he arrived.

"Oh, Mr. Mitchell?" Ms. Trout said as he reached the door.

"Yes?"

"Do you or your wife know a Mr. Achak?"

Doug's limbs went stiff. It was the last name he expected to hear at parent-teacher night. "Um…no, I don't believe so." He tried to think quickly. "Is he a teacher here?"

"No, but Janie's mentioned him more than once. Perhaps a neighbor?"

Doug acted as if he was searching his memory banks while secretly trying to find the words to end the conversation immediately. "Nope. Not on our street, anyway." He forced a smile, but it felt like a limp, lifeless thing on his face.

"Oh well," Ms. Trout said. "It's probably nothing."

Just as he was about to say something in response, Ms. Trout cut him off. "Good night, Mr. Mitchell."

He closed his mouth quickly and simply waved back.

When he arrived home, Janie was already in her bedroom. The door was closed and Carla noted she was playing with her dolls. When she asked about the meeting with Janie's teacher, Doug chose not to disclose the particulars. He simply told her that Janie's teacher was concerned about her performance on recent homework assignments. After more than one "I told you so!" from Carla, Doug conceded they would need to be more consistent with checking Janie's homework at night.

He'd already decided not to tell Carla about the discussion of Mr. Achak.

CHAPTER 8

By the time Doug returned home, the sun had already disappeared and the daycare kids were long gone; Carla typically shut down around four o'clock. Occasionally a parent would show up late, and if Carla liked the person enough, she wouldn't charge them extra. If the person was habitually late, then it was time for that individual to open the checkbook and pay the piper.

The meeting with Linda Trout had been a week ago, but the details of their conversation were still fresh in Doug's mind. He often thought about calling her, of asking her more about Mr. Achak. He thought about telling her what Janie had told him and Carla regarding the "other man" in the house. Ms. Trout might still be upset, but Doug could be charming. He could earn her sympathy and then she would listen.

As the days wore on, however, Doug decided it was best to simply move on. He didn't want to know more about the man of whom Janie spoke at home and in her class. He was sure he would learn more about Mr. Achak when Mr. Achak felt the time was right.

Doug walked in to an unusually quiet and calm house. That time of night, Janie would normally be sitting up on a stool at the bar, regaling her mom with stories about what happened at school that day while Carla prepared dinner—this tended to delay their meal more often than not. However, tonight, the table was set and dinner was served as he walked in the door. The breakfast bar stools were empty and Janie was absent.

He slid the straps of the backpack off his arms and set it on the floor against the bar. Carla stood in the kitchen with her back against the counter. One arm was folded across her waist, her hand tucked under her elbow, while the other hand held a near-empty glass of wine to her lips. Her eyes were somewhat narrowed, her gaze boring through him rather than *at* him. Doug could tell there was something wrong but he wasn't likely to be the source of her ire.

"So..." he started, "do I have to ask, or are you going to tell me?"

She pulled the wine away from her lips and swirled the glass, never once taking her eyes off him. She inhaled loudly, let out a long, controlled breath, and Doug gritted his teeth behind closed lips.

"Your daughter is in her room right now with the door closed."

"And...this is a problem?"

"She doesn't want dinner," Carla continued. "She's moody, she won't eat anything; she just came home from school, shut herself in her room, closed her window blinds, and hasn't come out since."

Doug slowly removed his shoes as he walked into the kitchen.

"Okay. That's unfortunate..." He spread his arms out wide in a gesture that said, "What do you want me to do?"

"I made pasta," Carla said.

Doug stopped and frowned. "Her favorite?"

Not only was it Janie's favorite dinner, she always helped Carla in the kitchen when her mother cooked pasta. Janie enjoyed testing the noodles to make sure they were done, checking to make sure they had that barely-crunchy, al dente perfection.

Carla nodded. "She said she's not eating tonight."

Doug sighed heavily as he moved through the kitchen toward the hallway. "Okay. I'll go talk to her."

He left the kitchen and reached her room; the door was still closed. Janie always played in her room with the door open. It wasn't an official rule, it's just how she always played. Doug listened at the door for a few seconds before entering. He could hear Janie talking, but he couldn't tell what she was saying. Her voice was naturally soft and delicate, so the door served as an effective sound suppressor.

As Doug turned the handle, he considered making the unofficial open-door policy in their home official.

Janie sat on her floor playing with her dolls. Doug smiled when he saw she had a Rapunzel doll in her hands while the others were simply laid out, scattered over her floor. He'd bought her Rapunzel from the local Target store a couple months ago on his way home from a long day at work. He had promised he'd be home in time to watch *American Idol* – their favorite show – with her, but after a series of long meetings forced him to break that promise, he'd lessened the sting by presenting her with the new doll.

"Hey, J-Bird," he said softly. "Feeling better today?"

"Hi, Daddy," she said without looking up. "I feel much better."

"That's good." He stood awkwardly with his hands in his pockets, looking around the room, but unsure as to why. "Do you want to come have dinner? Mommy made pasta!"

"Yes!" she said. She looked up at him and smiled brightly. He wondered if Carla had overstated Janie's behavior. This didn't sound like the same child Carla had described only a couple minutes ago.

"Get washed up and I'll see you at the dinner table." Doug left her in her room and walked back out into the kitchen.

Carla hadn't moved from where she stood. She silently asked Doug a question with her eyes. The glass in her hand was empty; translucent burgundy tears wept down the inside of the goblet. She'd recently taken her last sip.

"She's coming," Doug said. "And she seems pleasant enough to me." He continued toward the table and pulled out a chair.

"Right, because I made all that up when you got home," she said defensively.

Doug exhaled a defeated sigh. "She was probably just aggravated about something. Maybe a kid on the bus threw something at her; maybe her teacher yelled at her. We'll ask her."

Carla set the empty glass on the Corian counter and moved toward the table. "Well," she said, her voice sliding down to the calmer end of the scale, "you can ask her. She probably doesn't want to talk—"

Doug guardedly placed a finger over his lips and Carla stopped talking. He snapped his eyes left toward the hallway and back at Carla in the space of a nanosecond. Carla turned and saw Janie entering the kitchen.

"Hey, J-Bird," Doug said warmly. "You're just in time. Food's still hot."

Janie wordlessly approached the table. She lazily pulled out her chair and *thumped* down in her seat. Shoulders rolled, hands in her lap, she stared at her plate as if waiting for food to magically appear in front of her.

Doug shared a questioning glance with Carla and then reached for the tongs in the bowl of pasta. "Here, Sweetie," he said as he picked up her plate, "I'll serve you."

Janie sat still and didn't acknowledge his effort. She continued to stare at the space where her plate once lay. When Doug was done filling her plate with noodles, he extracted a ladle-full of sauce from another dish.

"Tell me when," he said as he poured red sauce on her pasta. Janie remained silent. Doug wondered what had changed in the thirty seconds since he'd visited her room and thought this was likely the same Janie Carla had welcomed home earlier. He flicked another glance at Carla. She raised a hand to her head, closed her eyes, and squeezed her temples.

After adding what he felt was a reasonable amount of sauce, Doug set down Janie's plate and proceeded to take some pasta for himself. He nodded toward a clear container with a green cap. "Cheese is right there if—"

"I don't want cheese," Janie said.

"—you'd like." Doug ignored her response and filled his plate. Then Carla did the same. The two of them began to eat, both pretending to be oblivious to Janie's behavior. She wasn't eating and continued to stare at her plate as if either entranced or brooding. Doug continued to eye Carla and saw that the fire in her eyes had begun to rage again. She stabbed at her meal and ate somewhat angrily, instead of slowly twirling her noodles like she usually does.

Doug turned to Janie. "Better eat up or it's gonna get cold."

"I'm not hungry."

Carla set her fork down roughly, the metal prongs *dinging* off the porcelain dish. It wasn't quite a *slam*, but it was far from gentle or meaningless. Her patience had just about run out and Doug was aware.

"Is it too much sauce?" he asked in an attempt to diffuse the situation before Carla had a chance to speak.

"I don't want it," Janie said.

"You know what, Janie?" Carla began, the venom on her tongue stinging even Doug's ears. "You'll eat your dinner, or you won't eat anything at all."

"*I don't want it!*" Janie yelled. She stood and kicked her chair backward, the wooden legs grunting against the floor.

"Hey!" Doug said, but she stomped from the kitchen and toward her room.

Doug rose from his chair and followed. "Janie, I'm talking to you!"

Just as he rounded the refrigerator, he saw the back of her head as she disappeared into her room. He walked to the door and saw her standing next to her bed. Her eyes were wide as he was about to enter and he noticed a touch of panic in her visage.

Then the door slammed in his face.

Doug fell backward against the opposite wall. Whether it was from the force of the door crashing against the jamb, or out of his own shock, he didn't know. And for about three seconds, he wasn't sure exactly what to do. When his mind caught up with the present, having already replayed what happened several times, he reached for the door handle. To his surprise, the door opened easily.

Janie stood by her bed. Her face was twisted in fear, and the tears had already started falling. Doug ran and dropped to one knee as he hugged her to him.

"Daddy, I'm sorry," she said through choked sobs.

"It's all right, baby. I gotcha. Daddy's here, Daddy's here."

Carla appeared in the doorway. "What the hell was—"

Doug held up a hand, dismissing any question Carla thought might have been important enough to ask. She eyed the doorway and then the door itself, perhaps looking for any kind of damage caused by the outburst.

"I think Janie's going to sleep in our bed tonight," Doug said to Carla. Then, turning to Janie, "Would you like that, Sweetie?"

Janie nodded. She buried her fists in her face, rubbed away the moisture that had softened and swelled the skin around her reddened eyes.

Doug looked back at Carla. She was no longer angry or frustrated. The only thing Doug saw in Carla now was concern. Perhaps even a bit of fear. Doug had no idea what was going on in their home and it appeared to him that Carla was also starting to think she didn't know either.

CHAPTER 9

Days went by, and soon another week. The three of them were cramped in Doug and Carla's queen-sized bed. For hours on end, Doug would roll and turn until he'd found a comfortable position, only to have it taken from him by a rogue elbow into his lower back, or a shoulder in his face. It seemed to him that every time he turned to face Carla, she was awake, staring back at him. The only one who seemed to be getting any rest was Janie, which was a good thing, but Carla and Doug quickly realized the new sleeping arrangement would need to end soon, nighttime visitors notwithstanding.

Doug was the first to say something.

"Janie, Mommy and I are going to sleep by ourselves tonight."

Janie played with her dolls in front of the TV in the great room. It was high-fashion week, apparently, as all her dolls were dressed in chic outfits with fancy sunglasses and tiny high-heeled shoes.

"Do you think you'll be okay sleeping in your room?" he asked.

Without looking up: "Of course, Daddy." Confidence, without even a thread of doubt or uncertainty held her words.

"Okay," Doug said, trying not to sound surprised and doing poorly at it.

"May I go to my room now?" she asked.

"Actually, why don't you go get washed up and brush your teeth? It's almost time for bed, anyway."

"Okay, Daddy." Janie stood and hugged him, her arms wrapped around his midsection. Doug felt silly as he held his arms out to his sides and didn't know what to do with them. Finally, he lowered them and embraced her upper shoulders.

"I love you, Daddy," she said.

He smiled. "I love you too, J-Bird."

Janie released her father and skipped out of the great room and toward the bathroom in the hallway.

In the kitchen, Carla finished packing the dishwasher and set the dial to ON. Doug walked up and rested a hand on the counter.

"Was that really that easy?" he asked. "Or did I just get played?"

Carla smiled. She looked off in thought of an answer. "I honestly don't know. I guess we'll find out tonight."

***

As he tried to sleep, Doug's thoughts were of coal stoves that fed themselves, and little girls who pretended to be asleep, or pretended to talk to invisible people. He thought of the door to Janie's room, slamming shut only inches from his nose. That was last week. Nothing had happened since. At least, nothing of which either Doug or Carla were aware.

Doug opened his eyes and stared out the bedroom window. There was a street lamp at the corner of their yard. Through the sheers it looked more like a soft, glowing orb. He stared long, watching as the light grew and contracted while his tired pupils dilated and narrowed. He was exhausted, but he wanted to stay awake as long as he could. He wanted to be conscious just in case anything happened. He didn't want to *allow* himself to fall asleep, voluntarily, for that would have been negligent. Rather, he wanted sleep to take him, to remove the burden of staying awake so he wouldn't have to give it up.

Eventually, the street lamp enlarged and brightened until Doug was no longer staring at it. He was now staring into the sun. He lay down on a beach under a blanket. To Doug, this felt awkward; normally, when he was at the beach, he sat on top of the blanket. But the cool beach air rolled across his face, over his body, and a warm, peaceful sensation radiated through him. He looked out into the water where Carla and Janie were playing in the surf. They splashed each other back and forth. He felt his lips stretch and curl upward at the corners. He touched his tongue to his upper lip and tasted salt.

Carla waved to him. He wanted to wave back, but he felt cozy and secure under the blanket. Janie waved, too. She wanted him to come into the water — Doug always played in the water with Janie.

He tried to get up, but the blanket held firmly. He tried to raise an arm to pull it down, but it trapped him like an iron cloth. Concern blossomed into panic, and soon he jerked his entire body, hoping to loosen the vice-like blanket as it had become rigid. He looked out into the water again and saw Carla and Janie laughing. They were no longer waving to him and no longer paying him any attention. They had returned to their ocean play.

Doug's panic soon escalated to complete hysteria. He yelled to them, but they did not hear. He couldn't hear his own voice. Other beachgoers walked by, around and in front of him. He screamed at every one of them, but they never heard his voice.

Suddenly, the blanket began to slide down off his shoulders and over his bare chest, moving along by itself.

Finally! He was going to get free!

The blanket slid down further and he was able to lift himself onto his elbows. He looked up and saw Carla and Janie staring at him from the water. They were no longer playing. They simply stood still.

Staring at him.

All the people at the beach had stopped moving and all eyes now covered him. Nobody said anything. Doug's fear rose once again as the blanket continued to pull away, and he wondered what would happen once it was pulled off completely.

***

Doug woke abruptly, his face sweaty and his heart racing. The heat in the room reminded him of the salty beach air he'd felt in his dream, but the blanket was gone and all that was left was the bed sheet.

Then, the sheet began to drift down his body.

He felt the cotton pass over his toes, like soft feathers tickling his lowest extremities. He glanced at the top of the sheet, near his chest. The sheet was slowly disappearing, moving down the bed. He looked over at Carla to see if she had moved, or was moving, or if she was pulling the sheet off the bed, but she lay perfectly still.

The sheet continued to move, dragged down and over his body by invisible hands. Now it passed his stomach. His waist. He watched the top of the sheet move across his upper thighs and toward his knees.

"Carla," he said, but his throat buckled and the word was barely audible, hardly a whisper. "Carla," he said again; this time his voice was clear. She opened her eyes.

"What? What is it?"

"Carla," he whispered. "The sheet...*it's moving!*"

Carla looked down and noticed her body was completely bare from her shoulders down to her waist.

The sheet pulled away fast and complete. Their bodies were completely exposed.

"Carla!" Doug yelled.

Then footsteps, fast and heavy on the floor, pounded near the bottom of the bed and headed for the door. Doug leaned in toward Carla, away from the edge of the mattress as the footsteps approached. He held out an arm, as if to shield Carla from some unseen force—some entity. The footsteps stopped.

The bedroom door, which had been ajar, opened slightly. There were a few aches and creaks in the floor as the steps turned soft and continued out into the hall. Then the door returned slowly to its previous position.

After that, the footsteps were no longer light; they hammered down the wood-floored hall. The weight of the being was palpable; the footsteps sounded like those of a grown man—a man the size of Doug.

The footsteps then stopped mere moments after they'd restarted, and Doug guessed them to have stopped near Janie's room.

He jumped from the bed; Carla was two steps behind.

They scrambled into the hall and hurried to their little girl's room. They pressed their ears to Janie's door and stared at each other in the dark, waiting to hear voices. Expecting to hear them. They both paused and held their breaths.

At first there was nothing. Not even a whisper. Doug knew what he'd heard, and by the look on Carla's face, she was aware some*thing* or some*body* was in the house, but he didn't want to charge into Janie's room out of fear of chasing away whatever it was that now lurked in the dark where his little girl slept.

Doug shook his head. Nothing. Carla nodded.

There was nobody in Janie's room.

Then a whisper from the other side of the door. Doug's eyes widened simultaneously with Carla's. It was Janie who spoke.

"I told you not to go in their room."

Doug felt all the warmth in his face evaporate, and replaced by ice and fear. He secretly hoped that, in the dark, Carla would be unable to see his new, pale visage. They waited to hear the voice. Not Janie's voice again, but the other voice…the stranger.

There was nothing.

And then:

"I like you. I just don't think *they* like you."

Doug had heard enough.

He opened the door and walked in casually, but with purpose, so as to appear confident, even though his feet barely lifted from the floor. He'd hoped the act had fooled Janie and whoever or *what*ever was in the room with her, because he hadn't fooled himself—certainly not when Carla bumped into him and stepped on his heels.

Janie was already sitting up in her bed. Doug hardly expected otherwise.

"Hey, Sweetie," he said in a soft voice. "Who're you talking to?"

"Nobody, Daddy. I was just having a dream."

Doug sat down on her bed. Carla stood against the opposite wall next to Janie's closet.

"What kind of dream?" he asked.

Janie looked down at her sheets and comforter. She twirled the corner of the sheet in one hand, stalling, as if thinking of a satisfactory response. "Just a funny dream," she said.

"Who was in your dream?" Doug pressed. "Was Mommy in your dream?"

She shook her head.

"Was I in your dream?"

She shook her head again.

Doug tossed a quick glance at Carla and caught her in mid-yawn. Had it not been two or three a.m.—whatever the hell time it was—he might have otherwise regarded her attitude as insouciant.

Even before he asked, he'd thought of the question already, days ago, probably even weeks. He assumed he would eventually ask, but hadn't brought himself to do it until now. He looked toward her window—at the moon's whitish glow against the back of her curtains. He had waited for something—a sign—to tell him *now* was the time to ask, and how to form the words. Would it scare her when he asked her? Would it scare Carla? For sure it would scare him, but he was long past the point of choosing abstinence.

"Was there a stranger in your dream?" he asked.

At this, Janie stopped twirling the sheet for a moment. She never pulled her head up, but even in the dark, Doug could see the bulbs of her retinas undulating beneath her half-opened eyelids as she again pondered the perfect non-answer. And then, she continued folding the sheet through her fingers.

"Yes," she said.

To the side, Doug noticed Carla's head tick up. If she was only semi-conscious a moment ago, she was fully alert now.

"Have you seen the stranger before?" Doug asked.

Janie nodded.

"Do you know his name?"

"I told you his name already. It's Mr. Achak."

"Oh." He delayed as he thought of something to keep talking. Then: "Is that the man who knocked the soda out of the fridge?"

She nodded again.

"Do you see him only in your dreams?"

"Sometimes I do."

"And sometimes you see him when you're awake?" he asked.

"I do. I think he likes it here."

Doug's heart thumped, a heavy pair of boots plodding quickly against the stairwell of his chest. Until now, he'd only assumed there was something going on in their home, something unnatural, out of the normal. Something *para*normal. But to finally hear the confirmation from his seven-year-old daughter left him with a feeling he hadn't expected: helplessness.

He felt naked and vulnerable. This thing, this entity inside their home, could see them all, but Doug could not see it. Likely, it knew where they were at all times, but unless it made a sound or showed itself—or pulled the sheets off the bed—he was completely unaware of its location in the house.

"Do you know why he likes it here, J-Bird?" Carla had finally joined the inquiry.

"I don't think he has a home," Janie said.

"Oh, that's sad," Carla said. "Isn't that sad, Daddy?" As she bore her eyes into his, through the veil that had lowered over his face after Janie had told them about the other man in the house, Doug snapped back; the veil lifted, and he was back in the conversation.

"So sad, J-Bird," he quickly added.

"Well," Carla said, "what if we let...Mr. Ahh-Shack...sleep downstairs?"

"In the cellar?" Janie asked, her voice colored a dubious grey.

"Sure," Carla said. "It's nice and dry, and Daddy keeps it warm. And it's dark down there, too, so he'll be able to sleep well."

Janie's mouth shifted to one side as she considered this arrangement. As she stared off, Doug cut a look at Carla. She responded by holding out her hands, palms up, as if to say, "You have a better idea?"

Janie then sat up straight and looked to the right of where her mother stood. Her expression was one of deliberation and she sat quietly for several seconds before answering.

"Mr. Achak doesn't want to go downstairs."

"Oh, no?" Carla asked. Janie shook her head. "Where would Mr. Achak like to sleep?"

"In the chair next to you, where he always sleeps."

Carla turned to the patterned glider. They'd held onto it ever since Janie was born. "Well, why do you think he wants to sleep right here?"

"Because he just told me," Janie said. "He's sitting in it now."

CHAPTER 10

A decision was made—primarily by Carla—to leave things alone. Doug was forced to try to ignore the man known as Mr. Achak, the random dialogues Janie would have with this unseen person, and the "bumps in the night," as Carla had so eloquently, and ignorantly, referred to them.

But Doug was unable to remain comfortable in their home. He wasn't even able to *achieve* comfort, never mind sustain it, and certainly not at night. Thoughts of a strange man, real or not, spending time in Janie's room (or in her mind) churned the bile in Doug's stomach into a stormy, raging sea. He hadn't expected to reconcile the idea of another man in Janie's life for at least another ten to fifteen years. And while this person wasn't made of flesh and bone, it still kept his little girl's mind occupied far more than he cared to accept.

During the nights, Doug would listen from his bedroom to Janie's voice as she spoke to the man she claimed inhabited her room with her. Occasionally, he would have to strain to hear, especially if her door was closed, which was now often. The only time Carla and Doug were ever able to leave her door open was after Janie had fallen asleep. Once they were certain she was unconscious, one of them would tiptoe down the hall and open her door, leaving it ajar. It wasn't ideal, but it was something.

Eventually, Janie was leaving *her* room in the middle of the night, walking into her parents' room, and waking Doug to tell him things like, "Daddy, Mr. Achak won't let me sleep," or "Daddy, Mr. Achak doesn't want me to go to school tomorrow," or "Daddy, Mr. Achak thinks you need to spend more time at work."

Janie's disposition had also begun to change dramatically. She'd shown only glimpses of the change when the activity had begun—mostly what Doug and Carla had passed off as mood swings. But where she was once perky and light-hearted, her demeanor had now turned sullen and melancholy almost full time. Doug couldn't remember the last time he'd seen Janie smile.

Once, while Doug and Carla were emptying the dishwasher, Janie's attitude took a most sour turn.

"This is getting ridiculous," Doug lamented as he raised a stack of dishes over his head and into a cabinet. It had been weeks since they'd eaten dinner together as a family.

"Well," Carla said, "at least she's not giving me sass anymore."

Doug stopped. "You don't see that as a problem?"

The TV in the great room had been left on and was airing the local news. The anchor was reading a story about recent power outages in nearby towns.

"What? Her not talking back?" Carla said. "I love it."

"Come on, you know what I mean. We always have dinner as a family."

"Maybe she's just going through her adolescent phase early," Carla said.

The local weatherman ran down the next morning's forecast.

"That's bullshit and you know it. This has nothing to do with adolescence. This has *everything* to do with whatever's going on in her room."

"Doug, she's not getting hurt. It's fine."

"Really? So you're not freaked out by all this?"

She sighed. "No, not really."

The meteorologist riffed a lame joke with the female anchor before sending the broadcast back to the desk.

"Well, maybe that's because it's me she wakes up every night to discuss the latest? I don't see her going to your side of the bed at three in the morning talking about how Mr. Achak wants me to spend less time at home."

"She said that?"

"Not her—Mr. Achak, apparently!"

Carla pursed her lips and Doug waited. Then, her face opened up into an "oh well" expression. "Hm, strange."

Doug stared at her. "Are you kidding me?"

The sound of a door opening halted their dispute. They both turned their attention toward the hallway where Janie had appeared. Without a word, she walked through the kitchen and into the great room. Neither Doug nor Carla spoke as Janie found the remote control and turned off the TV. She dropped the remote on the floor and walked back into the kitchen and headed toward her room.

"Why'd you do that?" Doug asked.

Janie stopped and turned to Doug. "TV is shit," she said. "Read a book or something."

Doug was too stunned to respond as Janie turned on her heels and continued toward her bedroom.

Carla exploded. "Wait just a goddamn minute, Janie!"

Janie stopped. Her eyes were dark, sleep-deprived orbs, and as she faced Carla, her entire body showed nothing but complete apathy.

"Who taught you how to speak like that?"

"Who cares?"

"I care! Tell me who!"

Janie let out an audible breath. After a few seconds of silence, she simply shrugged her shoulders.

"I don't *ever* want to hear that word out of your mouth again," Carla demanded. "Understand?"

"Sure."

"I mean it, Janie! Never again!"

Janie's and Carla's eyes continued to parry and joust. When it seemed like neither was about to concede the argument, Janie opened her mouth.

"Mommy, you need to loosen up. Maybe you and Daddy should get naked in your bed."

Carla's mouth hung open, too stunned to say anything. She and Doug stared at Janie as their daughter stood still, her face even and emotionless. Doug was nearly speechless as well, having swallowed hard before finally breaking the silence.

"Janie, go to your room," he said directly but calmly.

Without so much as a look in Doug's direction, Janie turned and left. Her door closed with a *click* and Carla broke down.

After the incident in the kitchen, Janie's afternoon routine became almost ritual: After the bus dropped her off, she would walk into the house, occasionally say hi to her mother, then head straight into her room and close the door. She would stay in there for hours, sometimes long after Doug got home from work, completely disengaged from her parents.

On nights she actually ate dinner, she would wait until Carla and Doug were finished before she came out of her room. She would then ask to sit at the table, alone, and eat her meal. How she ever knew they were done eating without coming out of her room first, they didn't know.

As this pattern of behavior carried on, Carla began spying on Janie, standing outside her bedroom and pressing her ear to the door. On every occasion, she would hear Janie talking. To whom, Carla didn't know. However, it wasn't simply idle chatter between dolls and toys; Janie was having actual conversations. The only problem was Carla couldn't hear the other speaker. And when she would ask Janie to whom she was talking, Janie would act like she hadn't spoken a word to anyone.

Doug heard the fear in her voice when Carla finally told him. She'd called him at his office while Janie was still at school, so he'd run into a nearby conference room for more privacy. There was a small table with four chairs and a single phone. The schedule posted outside the room indicated nobody had it reserved for at least another hour.

"What exactly did she say?" he asked.

"Christ, Doug, I don't know! I can barely hear her! It just sounds like a bunch of mumbling through the door!"

"Did you go in?"

A slight pause.

"I wasn't sure if I should."

Doug looked up as nosey co-workers peered through the windows of the conference room as they walked by. He ducked his head lower and pressed the handset to his ear.

Doug lowered his voice. "That's fine. What does it sound like? Can you make anything out?"

"Not really," she sighed. "At times it sounds like she's playing. Then other times it…"

"What?"

"It sounds like she's…fighting with someone."

"Fighting? How?"

"I don't know, Doug! I just hear her voice raise, like she's yelling at someone, but I can't make out her words."

"All right, I'm leaving now."

Doug arranged to leave work early so he could be home in time to hear these conversations for himself. After hearing the first one-way conversation, he'd arranged to leave work early a few more times. Several conversations later, it was obvious to Doug and Carla that Janie wasn't simply making up things to say, but that she was in fact *responding* to things being said to her.

It was after these conversations that Doug decided to invest in a digital voice recorder. A fan of many reality-based ghost-hunting shows, Doug assumed they would be able to record some of the activity. Carla, however, was not as easily convinced.

"What? EVPs, are you kidding?"

"What's the matter?" Doug appealed. "We can use it to see if there's anything going on in her room."

Carla was miles away from convinced. "You really think that's going to work? You really believe in that shit?"

He shrugged. "Who knows? Maybe it will catch something? And if it doesn't, then at least we tried."

"Doug, those shows are all fake. They only try to make you *think* you're hearing what they heard. None of that stuff works. You can't 'communicate with the other side!'" she exclaimed, using air quotes again.

Doug dropped the idea. Carla was either content to let things continue as they had been, or she was too scared to do anything about them. Either way, he knew it was a losing battle to try and convince her. He needed to talk more about what was going on, but he felt foolish discussing it openly with others. With limited options, Doug called his brother.

***

"Luke? Hi, it's Doug," he said into his cell phone. "What's up, man?"

It was Wednesday and Doug had caught Luke in between getting home from his part-time job and getting ready to go to his *real* job.

"What's going on, Doug? You at work?"

Doug had found a bench outside, far away from the main entrance and from the eager ears of his co-workers. The temperature was barely above freezing, but he wore a heavy, charcoal-colored pea coat that kept him warm.

"Yeah, I'm on break. Decided I'd give you a call. You busy?"

Luke let out a loud sigh, but not out of exasperation; he was a hard worker. "Nah, I just got back from a job with Timmy."

When not busy being an overworked police officer for an understaffed department, Luke worked part-time doing home remodeling with his friend, Tim. The pay was great, almost like a second salary, so a little fatigue during the day for an extra fat paycheck didn't faze him in the slightest.

"What's up? You sound tired."

"Yeah," Doug lamented. "I'm not getting much sleep these days."

"Uh-oh. Everything okay?"

"Yeah, I guess," Doug sighed.

Before dialing Luke's number, Doug had wondered how much he should tell him. Luke was four years older than Doug and not a believer in fantasy or the paranormal; he didn't believe in anything he couldn't see, touch, taste, smell, or hear. This belief had earned Luke many an argument over religion with their mother when he was a teenager.

"I've been meaning to ask you something for a while now," Doug said.

"What is it?"

"You remember Paul's imaginary friend?"

"Ahh," Luke said. Doug could sense his brother's smile through the phone. "Why, does Janie have a friend living in her room?"

"Yeah." Doug forced a laugh.

"Kinda weird at first, huh?"

"Seriously."

Doug tucked his free hand into his side as a cold wind passed through him.

"I wouldn't worry about it," Luke said. "Probably won't last long."

"How long did Paul's friend last before he grew out of it?"

"Damn, that was like twelve years ago," Luke said and tried to think back. "Probably about a year or two?" His voice rose in pitch on the last word, almost as if it was a question.

"Oh, Jesus!"

Luke laughed even harder. "It's all right. All kids have imaginary friends."

"I know. That's what Carla says."

"And I would believe her if I were you. She knows children. She's been teaching kids for how long now?"

"I know, I know," Doug relented. "This just feels…different."

"How so?"

After a few moments of hesitation, Doug decided to simply tip over the can and let its contents fall where they may.

"Weird shit's been happening inside our house."

Incertitude crept into Luke's voice. "Oh yeah?"

"I'm serious, dude," Doug protested. "Our coal stove has somehow been feeding itself during the night, soda bottles are jumping out of the fridge, doors are slamming by themselves, sheets are being pulled off me and Carla in the middle of the night—"

"Whoa, whoa, slow down man!"

"—and Janie tells us it's her friend, Mr. Achak, doing all this."

Doug caught his breath and waited for a response. He immediately regretted saying all that, but there was nothing he could do now. It was out there.

"Okay," Luke began. "So there's some wacky stuff going on in your house. What are you saying? There's ghosts in your house?"

"You know what... I shouldn't have said any of this." Frustration dripped from his words like blood from an open wound.

"I'm sorry," Luke said, laughing. "I'm sorry. But I mean, you call me in the middle of the day and throw ghost stories at me. What do you want me to say?"

"I know, I know. Like I said, I probably shouldn't have said anything."

Luke ceased laughing. "It's fine. Seriously. It's just unexpected. Tell you what: Mom and Dad are coming over this Saturday for dinner. Diane would probably like to talk to you. She loves this kind of stuff."

"Oh yeah?" Doug said.

"You guys should come," Luke urged him. "Diane's cooking. It'll be good."

Doug didn't hesitate to say yes. It had been weeks since he and Carla had any adult interaction, and they would benefit from having some contact with others. Janie would certainly benefit from having a little time with her cousins as well.

"Thanks, Luke." Doug said. "Oh, and do me a favor? Don't mention this to anyone yet?"

"Mention what?" Luke asked.

Doug grinned. "Thanks."

He said goodbye and closed his cell phone.

CHAPTER 11

Luke's wife, Diane, was the senior editor for a local newspaper. She was a conventional thinker, much like Luke, but she also had a curious streak when it came to things like what Doug and Carla were experiencing. Before taking the senior editor position, she once wrote a piece about an abandoned and allegedly haunted cemetery in a neighboring town. Many locals claimed to have seen a "white woman" on more than one occasion. Diane's motivation hadn't been to either glorify the legend or debunk an urban myth; she'd simply wanted to join the fun and try to have an experience, if possible. After a night spent with several other folks looking for a good scare, Diane swore her perspective on the paranormal had completely changed.

She sat next to a large, weathered tombstone. The moon was full and cast a bright light over the cemetery, but even the moonlight offered no help in reading the name on the marker. Her flashlight was also useless; the lines on the stone had faded away, erased by time and the elements. She opened a small legal pad and made a few notes.

"Whatcha writing, there?" the young man asked. Then his eyes lightened up. "You gonna mention us in your article?"

Scott Sweeney was a high school senior. He and his girlfriend, Rebecca Brown, were avid fans of all things paranormal. They frequented the cemetery with the hopes of seeing an apparition. Unlike most high school kids, who on the weekends opted to hang out with friends who had older brothers and sisters with access to alcohol, Scott and Rebecca spent most of their Friday and Saturday nights looking for the mysterious White Woman.

It is believed the spirit is that of a woman who died in a horrible car accident on the road that runs past the cemetery. Her young daughter also perished, but not at the same time; thus, their spirits were "separated." As a result, her spirit lives in a state of unrest as she searches for her daughter night after night.

Diane happened to catch Scott and Rebecca entering the cemetery just as she arrived. When she assured them she wasn't going to get them into trouble, Scott and Rebecca agreed to allow Diane to "hunt" for the White Woman with them.

"You guys think it's true?" Diane asked, ignoring Scott's question.

"Of course it's true!" Rebecca said. "Just because we haven't seen her doesn't mean it's not true."

Diane made a few more notes in her pad.

"So, do you, like, work for the paper or something?" Scott asked.

"Yep."

"I'm going to major in journalism!" Rebecca blurted out.

Diane smiled. *These kids are too cute.*

"That's great," Diane said, and she meant it.

Just then, Scott held a finger to his lips. His eyes scanned the surrounding area until they stopped at a point in the distance. He snapped his fingers and Rebecca stood up; she held a camcorder and pressed the Power button. A red light came on near the lens.

"I just saw some movement over there," Scott whispered. He motioned toward a large oak tree about twenty feet away.

The three of them stayed quiet, the only sound the hum of the camcorder. Diane strained her eyes to try to see what Scott saw. Between their position and the oak tree, there was another row of old headstones; some leaned over like the Tower of Pisa, some stood straight, and some were simply flat, brick-like stones sitting face-up in the ground.

A shadow passed in front of the oak tree.

"Did you see that?" hissed Rebecca.

"Shh!" Scott quickly shushed her.

Diane leaned in toward Rebecca, her voice low: "I saw it, too."

"I think we should go check it out," Scott said. He held out a hand. "Gimme the camera."

Rebecca turned it over to him and he led first. Then she followed.

Diane was last. She kept her eyes trained on the spot where she'd seen the shadow pass by. They moved slowly and quietly, walking almost in unison. Every few seconds, Scott would hold out a hand and they would stop. Diane wondered if he'd truly seen or heard something, or if he was simply showing off for her benefit. Regardless of the reason, she was as excited as they were and wanted to keep moving.

When they reached the tree, Scott squatted low to the ground.

"Okay," he said, his voice soft. "This is where I saw it pass by. Did you guys see it here as well?"

Diane and Rebecca nodded.

"Okay, cool. I think we should try to make contact."

Rebecca's eyes lit up and she smiled a toothy grin.

"How do we do that?" Diane whispered.

"Well, we can ask it questions," Scott said. "Going by the legend, of course. So, we can ask for her name, why she's here, if she's looking for her daughter—that sort of thing."

"Okay."

Scott turned to Rebecca. "Go ahead, babe. Ask a question."

Rebecca cleared her throat and asked out loud, "Are you lonely?"

Scott leaned in close to Diane, held the camera away, and whispered, "We probably won't hear anything, but if we get a response, it will come up on the camera's audio."

Diane nodded.

After thirty seconds of silence, Scott asked the next question: "Are you looking for your daughter?"

At first, there was nothing. Then, a branch above their heads crackled slightly. Rebecca's jaw dropped and her eyes went wide.

Scott shook his head. "Probably nothing," he whispered. "Just the wind."

They waited several tense moments for another noise, but the branch stayed quiet, along with everything else around them. Then, Scott gestured to Diane.

"Your turn."

"I'm not sure what to ask," Diane said.

"Just ask whatever comes to mind; whatever you want to know," Scott told her.

Diane thought long about it. At first, she didn't know what would be appropriate to ask. Then, she began to think of herself as the White Woman—a mother who had lost her child. As a young mother herself, Diane could only assume the depth of a person's anguish after suffering such a tragedy. The heartbreak of a loss so great couldn't possibly be measured. She started to think about what a person might do to eventually move on from this kind of agony.

She thought of her question.

"You've spent an awfully long time looking for your daughter," she said. "Did you ever think she might be waiting for you on the other side?"

Scott froze and stared at her. The words "holy shit!" formed on his lips, but he spoke nothing.

"Good job!" Rebecca whispered with an equal amount of encouragement.

Diane smiled, only slightly embarrassed to have received the proverbial "atta girl" from a couple high school kids.

The footsteps off to her left snapped her attention and her smile was quickly erased.

Scott aimed the camera in the direction of the sound. He held up a steady, leveled hand.

Don't move.

Another footstep fell heavily against the cold, solid ground. Diane's mind worked and she began to think she'd been conned.

"This is one of your friends, isn't it?" she asked.

Rebecca, with a tension-filled hand covering her mouth, shook her head. Even Scott's eyes were genuine.

Another footstep.

Diane whispered, "This is for real?"

Scott's arm began to slacken and he lowered the camera. "Oh my god..."

Diane finally turned to see what it was that had confounded Scott. Only five feet away, a whitish, semi-opaque, human-sized mass stood before her. Diane could not see a face or any limbs, but she could just discern a pair of shoulders and the round shape of a head. Based on the figure's posture, Diane surmised it was staring right at her.

A sporadic pounding of feet from behind spun her around. Scott and Rebecca had run for it. Diane was about to yell to them, but she heard the white figure take another step; she turned around just as she was knocked from her squatting position and onto her back. As she looked up, the white figure moved slowly over her. As it did, Diane felt an immense pressure against her chest; the pressure suffocated her lungs and she couldn't breathe. She tried to move her arms, but they, too, were pinned to the ground. Then, just when she was sure she was going to black out, the figure moved over her; the pressure released and she filled her lungs with air.

The figure kept moving and Diane pushed herself up onto her feet. She ran from the cemetery, to her car, and drove home.

CHAPTER 12

Dinner with Doug's family had been great. Diane may have been a talented writer and an exceptional editor, but she was a gifted chef. She came from a traditional Italian family that believed in big meals, family gatherings, and good food. She also came from a long line of great cooks and she was no exception. The roast beef tenderloin with homemade horseradish sauce was a revelation, one that Doug had enjoyed three times and almost a fourth when Carla grabbed the silver serving fork from his hand and said, "Save some for those of us who are starving!"

Christmas had passed over a month ago, but to Doug, it felt like the holidays all over again, having all his loved ones in the same place.

Luke and Diane had raised three wonderful children: Paul, who was fifteen; Sarah, eight; and Caleb, who was barely a year old. Sarah and Janie got along like two peas in a pod, genuinely enjoying each other's company. Being so close in age, they played with a lot of the same toys. They even traded dolls from time to time. Doug found it to be an odd activity until Carla asked him how many baseball cards he'd traded with his brothers when they were kids.

Doug's father, "Big Paul," after whom little Paul was named, had been telling him about his latest outing at the golf course. A former police lieutenant, the aptly named Big Paul—standing at six-feet, three-inches and weighing a svelte two hundred and twenty pounds—had retired two years ago and vowed never to work full- or even part-time again. He managed to stay in shape during retirement by running on a treadmill and lifting weights five days a week. He also spent three days each week playing in various golf leagues. Sometimes, on days he didn't have a match, he went and played, anyway. Doug's mother, Barbara, often joined him on those days. Unfortunately for Doug, he was *not* a golfer.

"I finally got your mother to hit from the men's tees today," his father said.

"Oh wow, really?" Doug did his best not to let his eyes gloss over and pass out on the floor in the dining room. "Isn't it a little cold to golf?"

"As long as there's no snow," his father began, "they'll open up. Sometimes they'll let you play the whole course...sometimes they close the greens...you know."

"Right," Doug agreed. He had no idea why people would want to golf in the winter.

"She hit very well, too. Kept it under a hundred. Couple birdies." He winked and nudged Doug's arm with an elbow that felt like a fifty-pound lead pipe. "That'll keep you coming back."

Doug sipped a seasonal beer and winced as Big Paul nudged him again. "Yep, that it will." Doug was just about to change the topic of the discussion to something mutual—the weather, taxes, or the upcoming baseball Spring Training—so as to preempt an inevitable golf-stance lesson, but Big Paul was too quick.

"I keep telling her," his father continued, "You can't force it, can't use too much right arm." He backed up and assumed a golfer's position, holding an invisible club out in front of him. "It's all in the backswing, in your approach. It's called, 'addressing the ball...'"

Doug's mind slipped under the sheets of apathy and he glanced off into the kitchen. He could see Diane washing dishes by herself and he secretly tried to think of reasons he needed to join her.

Diane's thoughts were of pleasant things—love, family, her children—as she rinsed a glass in the sink. She hummed a Kelly Clarkson ballad as she placed the glass onto the drying rack next to the sink. The words formed in her head: *I'll never stray too far from the sidewalk...*but not in her mouth, and the melody played on her closed lips.

She'd always enjoyed large family gatherings. Though the cooking was extensive, as was the cleanup afterward, she relished having all the people who mattered most under her roof at the same time. Her home was large, too, enough to allow for thirty to forty people to visit comfortably, with plenty of rooms and table space so nobody felt squeezed in.

As with most homes, her kitchen was always the most popular place. During gatherings like this, Luke, Doug, and Big Paul could often be found sitting at the breakfast nook and chatting about police procedures, or pouring shots of maple liquor. Yet surprisingly, she was currently the only one in there, as everybody else was enjoying either dessert or wine or beer. Or all three.

As she placed another dish on the drying rack, she felt a presence behind her and turned around. Janie stood there.

"Hi Janie," she said. "You surprised me! How long ya been standing there?"

"Hi, Auntie Diane." Janie stood with her hands behind her back and swayed back and forth. "I really enjoyed dinner."

Diane reached for the dishtowel on the counter, dried her hands, then tossed the towel over her shoulder. "Aw, thanks, Hon. That makes me happy."

Janie then went silent and her eyes darted left and right. Diane could tell Janie wanted to tell her something.

"Are you still hungry?"

Janie shook her head.

"Are you thirsty? There's water, there's juice…I think there's some milk left. Would you like some milk?"

Janie shook her head again. And then, as if prompted by a force unseen, she blurted out, "The black angel in Caleb's room doesn't like the alligator above his crib."

Diane tried to hold on to her smile and to ignore the punch of fear that had just connected with her chest. She was already aware of the situation going on at Doug and Carla's house—Luke had mentioned it to her after having spoken with Doug. But ever since her experience in the cemetery, Diane maintained a much different, more respectful attitude toward the paranormal.

Diane had never mentioned her experience with the White Woman to anyone, not even in her article. When the words escaped from Janie's mouth, the memory of having the air pressed out of her lungs nearly knocked her over. Janie had referred to the large, plush alligator that rested along the top of Caleb's crib. As to what relevance the alligator had to any supposed "angels" in his room, black, white or otherwise, Diane was unaware.

Several seconds had passed until she finally remembered to breathe. She spoke slowly to disguise the anxiety building within her.

"What angel, Hon?"

"The angel that lives up in the corner of his room," Janie said innocently. "He says the alligator is mean."

Diane didn't know how to respond. She could ask more about the angel, but she desperately wanted to discourage any further discussion about it. She decided to change tactics.

"You know, I think Caleb was looking for you earlier."

"He's only one," Janie asserted, referring to Caleb's age. "How do you know he was looking for me if he can't talk?"

"Umm..."

Think quick, think quick!

"I think he was crawling toward you earlier, just after dinner. I think he was trying to play with you."

"That's because the black angel was trying to chase him out of his room so it could get rid of the alligator."

Diane felt lightheaded. "He...he was chased away...by the angel?"

From where he stood in the dining room, Doug saw movement in his periphery: Janie had just walked into the kitchen and appeared to be talking with Diane. Janie's back was to him, so he couldn't see her face, but her body language appeared easy, friendly. Diane's countenance, however, pallid and fearful, suggested to Doug that Janie's discourse was anything but light.

Doug turned to his father, who'd been describing a rather challenging wedge shot (most of which Doug hadn't heard), and excused himself from the conversation. He then quickly slid into the kitchen.

"Hey, girls," he said lightly. "Hope I'm not interrupting anything. Any dishes left that I can help with?"

Janie turned and said, "I was just talking with Auntie Diane, Daddy."

"Oh yeah? What were you talking about?" He glanced subtly at Diane and returned his eyes to Janie. In that briefest of looks, he saw concern on Diane's face. Concern that bordered on panicked terror.

"We were talking about Caleb!" Janie said happily. She was completely oblivious to Diane's reaction to her previous disclosure.

"Oh, that's great!" Doug said. "Because he's in the great room and he keeps looking around. I think he's trying to find you."

"Okay!" she said, and skipped out of the kitchen.

He watched her leave; without turning around, he said quietly, "You two weren't talking about Caleb, were you?" After no response, he turned around and saw a tear fall down Diane's cheek. She brushed a hand across her face, smearing the wetness.

"Doug, is this for real?"

He played dumb. "Is what for real?"

She stared into his eyes plainly. "Doug, Luke told me what's been going on."

"He did, huh?" Doug asked. He nervously scratched the back of his head as he walked across the kitchen to the small, round breakfast nook and pulled out a stool. He uttered a heavy sigh as he sat down. "What did Janie say?"

"I'd rather not repeat it," she said. She pulled out the other stool and sat cater-cornered. "I know you said she talks about these things but..." She let her arms fall on the tiled surface of the table and expressed concern with open palms. "Is this *really* real? I mean, is she in any danger? Is Caleb in any danger? What's happening? Is it—"

Doug cut her off and rested a hand in hers.

"I'm so sorry, Di," he said. "I never intended to scare you. I didn't want to get anyone involved but..." He looked around to make sure nobody else had entered the kitchen. "Carla and I aren't seeing eye-to-eye on this one."

Diane sniffed and dabbed her eyes with a napkin. "What does she think?"

"She thinks it's weird as hell," he said matter-of-factly. "But since Janie's not getting hurt by this...whatever it is, Carla just thinks it's something she'll grow out of."

"Okay," Diane began, "so she's not getting hurt physically. But how is it on her mentally? Emotionally?"

Doug shrugged.

"How's she doing in school?"

"Ha..."

"That good, huh?"

"I met with her teacher already." He looked down and absently scratched where the tile met the wooden edge of the tabletop. "She thinks Janie needs some kind of 'special education.'"

Diane sighed. "That's bullshit, Doug. Don't listen to that."

"I know, I know." He studied his fingers as they traced along the grout between the tiles. "I just don't know what else to do. That's why I called Luke."

"Well, I think we can both say this is beyond Paul's imaginary friend experience."

"Mm," Doug offered. He continued running his fingers over the grout lines. Then, he said, "I have to admit, you seem a lot more frightened by this than I expected."

Diane hesitated at first, then she told him about her experience in the cemetery. Everything from the White Woman to the high school kids to the apparition...she spared no detail.

"Holy shit," Doug said quietly.

"Yeah, tell me about it."

"I had no idea. I mean, I knew you were interested in this stuff but..."

"Oh, I am," Diane said, "but that experience taught me a lot. About respecting the dead, the paranormal...about everything."

Doug nodded slowly. They both sat quietly, letting the silence drape over them like camouflage, as if the situation wouldn't exist if they simply stopped talking about it.

Then Diane asked, "Does she talk to it?"

"Huh? Oh, Janie...yeah, all the time."

"Have you thought about recording it?"

"Funny you should ask. Carla and I talked about that the other day."

"And?"

"She's not a fan of the idea."

"Well, you'll just have to give her time and try to convince her. It may not appear this is as hard on her as it is on you, but she's strong; she keeps her emotions hidden. I'm sure it's tearing her up inside."

"Yeah, I know."

"Well, keep trying. She loves Janie just as much as all of us. I'm sure she'll come around."

"I will. Thanks, Di."

She reached across the small table and rested a hand on his shoulder.

"You know, girly," Carla began as she entered the kitchen. "If I didn't trust you, I'd think you were trying to steal my man away from me." Her smile was enormous; infectious. She was clearly teasing them.

Diane didn't miss a beat. "Any time you wanna play 'switcheroo,'" she said, swinging her index finger in a small circle, "you just let me know."

"Damn, girl!" Carla held up an empty wine glass. "Do I need to cut you off?"

Diane winked at her and they both laughed. Doug looked up at Carla and smiled sheepishly. She studied his face, but before she could ask, Diane spoke.

"I was just consoling your man here; he'd just been put through the ringer with your father-in-law."

"Oh, boy," Carla lamented. Then she dropped her voice to a near-whisper: "Not another 'eighteen-holes-of-hell' again?"

Doug only smiled back at her.

CHAPTER 13

The drive home was quiet, which was fine with Doug. He'd done enough talking throughout the evening. He stared at the road ahead, at the double solid yellow line; then a broken line; then one solid and one broken. From the corner of his eye, he could tell Carla was anxious. He was sure he knew the reason why, but he was more interested in studying traffic lines and street lamps than any further discussion of their current struggles at home. He noticed only some of the street lamps were on and seemed to be alternating...the first would be on, but the next would be off. On...off.

Why do they do that?

"So..." Carla said, cutting the silence. "Are you going to tell me what you and Diane were *really* talking about tonight or what?"

"It's nothing," he said. He scratched at his head, just behind his ear.

"Doug, I can tell when you're lying. You do that thing where you scratch your head."

"That's not true," he said. "I only do that when I'm uncomfortable."

Carla bellowed out a short, mock laugh. She looked over at him, but Doug stared ahead. He gave her a quick whale-eye glance and she caught it.

"So, you told her, huh?"

"Actually, I told Luke. *He* told Di."

"Well," she sighed, "I guess it was just a matter of time before people found out."

Doug only nodded.

"What did she say?"

Doug regaled her with his and Diane's discussion. He mostly kept his eyes on the road, but glanced over at her from time to time. Her eyebrows narrowed occasionally and she nodded along quietly. This was a good thing, Doug realized, as it was better than getting chewed out for letting other people know about their issue. Carla hated airing dirty laundry, even to family.

When he was done, he let the after-silence hang in the air for a bit and waited for her to respond. Carla turned toward the back seat; Janie was passed out, her head resting against the window.

"I guess it's a good thing Di doesn't think we're crazy," she said.

"Yep," Doug confirmed.

"What did she say when you mentioned the voice recorder?"

He hesitated for a bit. Doug was well aware of Carla's deep respect for Diane's opinion on just about everything, but he didn't want her to think he was using that faith as part of his argument. After a few seconds' pause, he casually said, "She thinks we should give it a shot."

Carla nodded some more, then stared ahead through the windshield. Doug knew she wasn't looking at anything, but rather absorbing everything he'd said. At this point, he'd already claimed victory since she hadn't refuted or argued with any part of his and Diane's conversation.

After a few more moments of contemplated silence, Carla simply said, "All right."

Doug's eyes left the road as he glanced at her quickly. "Does that mean you want to go for it then?"

"Sure," Carla sighed. Then her tone turned a little strict. "I just don't want you to turn this into some kind of experiment."

"Won't happen," he said, making a short up-and-down slicing motion with a flat right hand. "I promise."

"I don't want you to force Janie to talk to this...whatever it is."

"You have my word."

"I'd prefer she doesn't even know it's there."

"I was thinking of hiding it high up on her shelf," Doug explained further. "The one that holds that snow globe she got from my mother for her birthday."

"Yeah," Carla said. "That's fine."

"Cool." He glanced over at her again and saw a flat smile on her lips. "Thank you."

Carla let out a harrumph, then said, "Let's see what kind of ghost hunter you are."

CHAPTER 14

"So all I do is slide this lever, push this button to select a new file, and then the red button records?"

Doug held a small device in his hand — a digital voice recorder.

"That's pretty much it," the young salesman said.

Doug wondered how much a teenage kid working part time for minimum wage in a national electronics chain store could possibly know about voice recorders. Along with recording the activity in the house, Doug figured he'd be able to use the device at the office to record meetings, conference calls, candidate interviews and then some. Surely the kid had never attended such a gathering. How much could he really know about these devices?

"Pretty much?" Doug asked doubtfully.

The kid briskly — and confidently — took the device from Doug's hand and began to operate it as if it were his own. He flipped the switch that apparently turned the device on, pressed a button, then another button, then said, "Ready?" Doug nodded absently and the kid pressed the red button in the center. He then held the device chest-high.

"This is Ryan and I'm standing here with…" He stared at Doug and waited for him to respond.

"Oh, uh, Doug."

"…at the Westfield Mall looking at voice recorders, trying to decide which one makes the most sense for recording 'bored' meetings." He glared at Doug. "That's B-O-R-E-D, not B-O-A-R-D."

Doug felt his face flush.

"We're particularly interested in model M-X-T-dash-one-zero-zero. Doug, what are your thoughts on this machine?"

The kid was good. He had to give him that. And in spite of himself, Doug almost laughed.

"Doug? Your thoughts?"

Oh shit, he's serious.

"Umm, I think this is a fine choice, Ryan." Doug spoke loudly and over-enunciated every syllable. A few customers turned to see who was shouting in the store.

"Just speak normally, Doug," Ryan said softly, almost in a whisper. "This is just a test. Go ahead."

Embarrassed, and of the sudden realization that Ryan had sized him up just as quickly as Doug *thought* he had sized him, he gave it another try. He noticed Ryan still held the device close to his own body and didn't extend it to Doug.

"I think this is a very good model, Ryan." His words came out naturally and his voice was at a comfortable volume. "And I appreciate your level of service and dedication to your product knowledge." He winked.

Ryan smirked and chortled. He tapped the red button again and immediately pressed play. Doug was amazed at how clear the sound was. Not only were his and Ryan's voices incredibly present and articulate, he could even hear the faint *beep-beep* and *ching* of cash registers in the background. Doug was aware the registers were at least thirty yards from where he stood.

"Damn," he said.

"I know," Ryan offered. "I use this model to take notes when I feel like dozing off in my European History class." He winked at him and it was now Doug's turn to laugh.

"Nice work," he said.

Ryan shrugged and his eyes went upward in a gesture that said, "Aww shucks, Mister, it was nothing."

Doug drove straight home after he left the store. It was still the middle of the day—he had left work early in order to plant the new device in Janie's room before she got home from school. He still planned to hide it on the high shelf, far out of her reach and line of sight.

It was a fairly simple little machine; a name brand, but not top of the line. For his application, Doug only needed something that recorded and played back. The kid from the store had rattled off different options like "expandable storage," "track mark function," and "dictation correction function," which had been his favorite.

In the end, he decided on a Sony that cost under thirty dollars. Doug had considered even that a bit pricey, but Ryan had reminded him, "In this day and age, you get what you pay for."

Pretty bright for a teenager.

When he arrived home, it was only one o'clock. The daycare kids were still there but Janie wouldn't be home for at least an hour and a half. He'd be able to hang out in the study, away from the children, and practice using the device.

Carla was busy feeding snacks to the kids as Doug walked in the door. Apparently, one of the little boys didn't have any snacks—likely thanks to a parent who had forgotten to pack such important items—and Carla was busy teaching the kids about the virtue of sharing. She never broke from teacher-mode as she passively waved to Doug on his way through the kitchen and down the hall.

When he reached the study, Doug set his backpack on the floor and removed a white plastic bag from inside. From the plastic bag he removed the voice recorder package and sat down at his desk. He struggled a bit with the clamshell packaging until the joints finally separated and the device fell into his hand. He found the Power lever on the side and slid it upward, the same way Ryan had showed him. On the device's small screen, about one square-inch in size, Doug saw a list of options. He selected the New File option and pressed the red Record button and the numbers started counting upward. He brought the voice recorder a couple inches from his mouth but then, remembering Ryan's demonstration from the store, he instead set the recorder on his desk. He spoke:

"My name is Doug Mitchell and this is my first recording." He paused, not knowing what else to say. He looked around, at the dark mahogany bookshelf standing against the wall, and the small end-table and the stained-glass lamp. "I am in the study of our home. So far, none of the activity seems to have taken place in here." Another pause, and then, "At least, not to our knowledge." He thought about saying more, but then ended the recording with, "This is the end of session one, Doug's study."

He pressed the red button again and the recording stopped. He then pushed Play. As he listened to his voice speaking back to him, Doug found the device worked just as well as the store model. Ryan knew his shit. The kid was also correct in that the device was simple to use. Doug had all the functionality he would need.

Dictation correction, my ass.

He stood from the desk and picked up the recorder. He used one of the arrow buttons to locate the file he'd just recorded and deleted it. He then left the study and headed toward Janie's bedroom, which was a mess and expectedly so. Not too many seven-year-olds clean their rooms before school, and since Carla had her hands full with the daycare most of the day, Janie's room usually only saw a pick-up on the weekends.

As he walked across the floor of her room, Doug navigated around dolls—everything from American Doll to Barbie to Bratz—toed between plastic toy kitchenware, sneakers that had been either worn or tried on and then discarded, and other articles of clothing. He sat down on her bed, careful not to further disturb the unmade comforter. Janie wasn't one for making her bed, either. But again, that would happen on Saturday. Or Sunday.

Doug's eyes wandered the room. He tried to imagine what it might be like to sleep there, only to wake up and see a stranger standing over you. Granted, he wasn't certain this is exactly how it happened with Janie. In fact, if he believed her account, the stranger usually sat and slept in the chair positioned in the corner opposite her bed.

He shivered as he thought about it. He couldn't imagine what she must be going through. How a seven-year-old girl could ever manage to be this tough and determined in the face of the unknown was both impressive and sad. He silently said a prayer, hoping that he would also show the same level of fortitude if and when he ever got to see this person—this entity, rather—up close. He stood and moved toward the shelf by her window.

He reached the shelf on top of which sat several framed pictures of family outings and events, as well as a beautiful snow globe featuring a frozen-in-time miniature of North Conway, New Hampshire—a favorite winter vacation spot of Doug's parents. He shook the globe. It required a turn of the crank for the trinket to play its song, but a simple shake was enough to create a squall. Snow swirled around, storming over the quaint, eclectic town with the fantastic skiing and wonderful eateries. He set the snow globe back on the shelf and hid the recorder behind a nearby picture frame. At five-foot, ten-inches, it was an easy reach for Doug, and probably just as easy for Carla, who stood six inches shorter than him. For Janie, however, it would be impossible. For one, she wouldn't be able to see it. For another, even if she *could* see it, she wouldn't be able to reach it. Even if she stood on the chair in her room, she'd still be a few inches short.

Doug looked at his watch and when he saw it was almost two p.m., he wondered where the last hour had gone. Still, there was plenty of time. Assuming Janie would head to her room immediately upon arriving home, Doug wanted to make sure the device was already recording so he didn't have to run into her room and risk having to make an excuse if she caught him in there. Also, the device could record over one hundred hours continuously in a single file. Thirty or forty minutes of lead-time would hardly put a dent in the machine's capacity.

He leaned close to the shelf, pressed the Record button, and walked out of the room.

Janie walked in just before two-thirty. Doug was in his study preparing a presentation for work. He'd regretfully opined a bit too loudly (and too frequently) at a recent meeting regarding a particular business process. In the end, he'd been tasked with identifying all the flaws with the current process and designing a new one that would not only improve upon those flaws, but also make his department more efficient in terms of workflow and resources. Doug's manager had asked him to provide what, in his opinion, would amount to a "blue sky scenario." In the last thirty minutes, Doug had completed the title slide of the presentation.

Janie appeared at the edge of Doug's vision, standing in the open doorway to the study.

"What are you doing home?" she asked wide-eyed, lips curved into an open-mouthed smile.

"Surprise!" Doug said. He stood and spread his arms. "Come give Daddy a hug!"

Janie ran to him, the straps of her backpack clinging to her bent elbows. When she came to him, she reached her hands as far as she could, but the straps prevented her from giving a proper hug. They both laughed as she did her best robot, walking straight-kneed and moving her restricted arms in a mechanical fashion.

"How come you're home so early?" she asked.

"I just felt like leaving early today," he lied. "Why don't you go put your backpack in your room and then we can go play?"

"Okay!" she beamed and left the room just as robotically as she had come in.

Strange, Doug thought. *Carla says she's always a bear when she gets home...*

He wondered if anything had been different between today and any of the days before; perhaps it was simply his presence.

Doug continued work on his presentation and prepared to shut down his laptop upon Janie's return. After a few minutes had passed, he started to wonder what delayed his daughter. He assumed she would be right back after she'd put her backpack away, but clearly she wasn't in any hurry to play.

A door opened in the hallway. Surely it was Janie's door, as her room was next to Doug's study, but he realized he hadn't heard her door close earlier. He paused at his computer, listened to the creak of the wood floor as soft footfalls approached the study. There was a loud *crick* from one of the floorboards just before she reached the doorway. Then she was there, staring at him.

"What's this, Daddy?" She extended her hand, exposing a small, silver object. Doug recognized it immediately.

That's impossible.

It was the digital voice recorder.

Doug struggled for an answer. The air was sucked out of his lungs and his stomach pressed against his lower abdomen. Even when he tried to stall by saying, "Umm," all that came out was a breathy, crackly, "ugghk…"

"Daddy?" she pressed.

Doug swallowed hard, found his voice. "Yes, Sweetie?"

"This was in my room." Her voice was flat. Not accusatory, but Doug couldn't help but feel he was on trial for a crime he'd committed.

He felt defenseless being interrogated as he sat behind his desk. He stood from his chair. His legs were weak but he decided to walk to her anyway.

"Where did you find that?" he asked, attempting to keep a steady, even-but-pleasant tone. He turned up his palm and she placed the voice recorder into it.

"Mr. Achak wants to know what it is," she said, ignoring Doug's question. "I told him it looks like an iPod, but he said he doesn't know what an iPod is. What is it?"

He wasn't sure how or when it happened, but Doug suddenly felt inferior to her, as if their roles had been reversed. He was now the guilty child being passively scolded by the adult. He cleared his head of the implication and forced his mind to work quickly.

"It *is* an iPod," he stammered. "I must have left it in your room when I got home from work."

"Really?" she asked. "It looks different from a regular iPod. What do those buttons do?"

"You know what," Doug began, "why don't you get some homework done and then help mom with dinner?"

As if entranced, Janie remained still and stared at him. "Daddy…"

Doug cleared his throat. "Yes, Sweetie?"

"How come you were in my room?"

Shit. Think, think, think.

"When I got home, I noticed one of the power lines outside was low and I wanted to get a better view of it from your window."

"Why didn't you just go outside and look?"

SHIT!

Her expression was dead. Not a single muscle contracted in her face and she hardly blinked. He felt increasing warmth near the front of his shirt, felt it crawl up his neck, into his face and around his ears. He was red. He knew it. And she simply stood in front of him. Still. Poised. Unwavering.

She stared up at him, her eyes demanding a response that wouldn't come. For a moment, Doug thought she might be controlling the redness in his face through some kind of telepathy.

Then she asked, "What's in my room, Daddy?" It was a rhetorical question; Doug knew as much.

You know damn well what's in your room.

He wanted to leave the study, the house, the yard. He wanted to go somewhere he didn't have to have this conversation. He wanted to go where it was three months earlier and none of this shit had happened yet.

He glanced down at his hand, uncurled his fingers and looked at the voice recorder. He could barely see the numbers as they counted up due to the blanket of moisture left by the sweat from his palm. He was trapped.

"Can I have my room to myself now?" She was direct and persistent.

Doug nodded weakly. "Sure, Sweetie," he managed to say. "Sure."

Janie turned slowly and walked out the door.

Doug placed a hand against the wall and exhaled a long, silent breath. A few more breaths and he could feel the heat starting to leave his face.

Out in the hall, Doug heard Janie's bedroom door close.

CHAPTER 15

Over the next few days, Janie continued her routine of coming home from school, going to her room, closing the blinds and the door, and talking (ostensibly to the entity) for hours. The voice recorder had sat in the top drawer of Doug's desk ever since he'd finished brooding over his failed attempt to record Janie in her room. He was still confused as to how she'd seen or found it on the shelf. She didn't have a stool in her room and her bed was too far away for her to stand on; there was no way she could have reached it without...assistance. The idea of some unseen being pulling it down from the shelf and handing it to her had entered Doug's mind, but he'd immediately pushed it away.

He'd been defeated. Janie had foiled Doug's idea entirely and fairly. He wasn't confident that another EVP attempt would succeed, so he needed a different approach.

Although their home had been built in 2001, Doug was aware the property had once been owned by and lived on by someone before him and Carla. He also knew another house had once stood in the near-exact location of their home, but had no knowledge of who the person or persons were, how long they'd lived there, or what had happened to the house. Doug had assumed a fire; otherwise, why knock down a perfectly good home?

Doug had heard theories about spirits who were unable to rest after suffering a violent or unexpected death. He wondered if something like this was happening now on his property. Perhaps the previous landowner (or owners) met an unfortunate fate that somehow "woke" a restless spirit when he and Carla built their home on the property. But they had built their home years ago. Why now?

Standing in the floral wallpapered kitchen of his neighbor, Wayne, Doug asked him if he knew anything about the previous landowner.

"No idea, man" Wayne said bluntly.

Wayne Sears and his wife, Melinda, had moved into the area several years before Doug and Carla built their home. Wayne, a full-time construction worker, and Melinda had moved up from Tennessee. His company had won a bid to build a series of bridges in western Massachusetts. The project would end up taking almost a decade to complete. He and his wife had fallen in love with the area when they first moved, and since they had no children and no familial ties left in Tennessee, they decided to stay in Massachusetts when the project was finished.

Wayne was older than Doug by twelve years, but his maturity level was roughly that of a teenager—he'd never graduated high school. He had a big heart, though, one he often wore on his sleeve, and Doug was happy to call him a neighbor as well as a friend.

Wayne offered Doug a beer and they sat at the Sears' large oak table in their kitchen. In certain company, Wayne was painfully aware of his lack of education and often used alcohol to avoid seeming unrefined over the course of any heavy discussion. In Doug's company, however, beer was simply a common denominator—they both enjoyed a good craft brew.

"When we moved in, there was nothin' there," Wayne said about the property.

"Nothing at all?" Doug asked.

Wayne tipped the bottle against his lips before taking a long sip.

"Well," he said, and pointed over Doug's shoulder with the hand that held the beer. "You could tell there was a house or sump'm there, the way the land was perfectly flat. Seemed like there was a faint outline of where the old foundation used to sit."

"Yeah. Ours was brand new. New concrete, new footings...they told us none of the previous foundation remained in the ground. Doesn't that sound strange?"

"Eh, a little bit." Wayne took another sip, pulled the bottle away, and briefly studied the label. Then he motioned to the beer in Doug's hand. "What do you think?"

"It's good. Where's it from?"

"I think upstate New York."

"Oh, like Saranac?"

"Pfh, nah, this is better'n that shit."

Doug laughed. He knew Wayne's most despised brew came from the Utica-based brewery, but any time Doug mentioned it to Wayne, it was like the first time. Whenever they drank, Doug would strategically try to bring it up—an inside joke only he enjoyed. Doug often wondered if Wayne had caught on years ago and simply continued to play along, or if he'd yet to recognize Doug's ruse.

"So why're you askin' about yer property now?"

Doug's eyes went to the floor and he coyly said, "I'm just curious about the land. Just felt like finding out who lived here before and what they were like." He looked back up at Wayne, studied his face to see if he was buying any of it. "Nothing important, really. Just curious."

Wayne nodded slowly, nursed another sip, and Doug immediately kicked himself for not telling the truth.

Come on, man, you came over here for a reason.

"Actually," Doug started, "I am kinda interested in something specific."

"What's that?"

"You ever heard of the name 'Achak' before?"

Wayne chortled. "Isn't that that test with the spots that look like coffee stains on paper?"

Doug smiled. "Nah, you're thinking of Rorschach."

"Right!" Wayne said as he pounded a proud fist on the table. "Everybody sees sump'm different and what YOU see says sump'm weird about ya, right?"

"Yeah," Doug said. "Something like that."

"Dang, I can't believe I got those two mixed up."

The two of them paused a few moments before Wayne spoke up again.

"Is this Achak fella the guy who used to own yer property?"

"Well, it's hard to explain," Doug said. "There's just been some weird shit going on lately."

A wry smile crept across Wayne's lips "You mean like ghost shit?"

Doug shrugged and tried to deflect by taking a long sip from his beer. "Eh, I don't know. Maybe…"

"Ha!" Wayne shouted, smacking the edge of the table again. "I knew it! It's ghost shit, isn't it? What's goin' on over there? Are the lights flickerin' when they shouldn't?"

Doug forced a laugh and he heard the apprehension slip out of his mouth. "Nothing's going on, man. I was just curious." He took another long sip.

"Yeah, right," Wayne said. "It's all right, you can tell me. I'm not gonna laugh at ya. Anymore."

Doug watched Wayne tighten his jaw as he tried to force his mouth from forming another inevitable grin.

Doug sighed. "Just a few things have happened, that's all. I'm not about to call Ghost Busters, if that's what you're thinking."

"Haha!" Wayne bellowed out. "Don'cha feel better now that ya told me?"

Doug simply shook his head and stared at him through narrowed eyes as he took another swig off the beer.

"Oh!" Wayne's face suddenly lit up, his eyes as big as golf balls. "Ya know, that woman on the other side of ya has been here a looong time."

"Who, Esther?" Doug asked, referring to the woman whose property neighbored his on the opposite side.

"Yeah, her," Wayne said. "She's been there for years. She might know who used to live there."

"Cool. I'll see what she has to say." Doug tapped Wayne's bottle with his own. "Thanks, buddy."

"Anytime," Wayne said.

As Doug stared out the back window of Wayne's kitchen into the woods behind their homes, he saw Wayne's face turning red from the corner of his eye. When he turned to him, Wayne looked ready to burst out in laughter.

Those Among Us

"Good luck, ghost wrangler!" Wayne laughed at himself.

Doug smiled and embarrassingly shook his head. The conversation hadn't been exactly what he had expected—truly, he wasn't sure *what* to expect—but the brief levity he enjoyed with Wayne was much needed.

After he finished his beer, Doug left Wayne's house and walked across his front yard over to Esther Bromley's home. She lived in a small cape, smaller than Doug's ranch and made of brick. The home retained a very rustic, old school New England charm, since most houses on Doug's street had gone to vinyl siding.

His gaze wandered across the road and up the street where the new shopping plaza was nearly finished.

What a freaking relief it will be once all this crap is done.

Peace and quiet had moved away from his block as soon as the heavy machinery moved in. Luck was marginally on Doug's side as he only had to endure the sounds—the *clangs*, *bangs* and diesel engines—two days out of each week. Fortunately, the contract, as he'd discovered after talking with Wayne, did not include hourly wages for the workers. They had a deadline to meet, so the project would need to be completed sooner rather than later. Unfortunately, this meant the contractors worked weekends, and the crews usually started at seven a.m.—even on Saturdays and Sundays.

Doug reached Esther's driveway, saw her blue '93 Ford Escort parked at the top, and proceeded to the front door.

Doug looked down at the concrete steps in front of the house. They were old and weathered, having cracked and separated from the home's foundation many years ago and were never repaired. But the old woman did her best to class things up, if only slightly. She'd placed small flowerpots on the edge of each step, assumingly to disguise the decrepit stairs with bright reds, yellows, and purples. Unfortunately, since it was winter, the pots now held nothing but dirt and the wilted remains of what were once flowers.

Doug rapped his knuckle on the glass of the storm door. From inside, he could hear the rickety springs of an old recliner argue and moan; she'd perhaps been watching TV, or maybe enjoying the latest *Reader's Digest*. Doug heard Esther's slow, shuffling footsteps as she approached the other side of the door. When it opened, it did so slowly.

Esther Bromley opened the door with her right hand; her left rested on a cane. She wore a light blue muumuu with a paisley pattern and squinted through the door at Doug as he stood on the steps outside. Her white hair was curled and matted, as if she hadn't bothered to fix it since she woke up that morning.

"Hi, Mrs. Bromley," he called out, unsure as to why he was talking so loud. The woman was old, not deaf. "It's Doug, from next door."

"Oh, hello, Doug. Would you like to come in?" Her voice rolled like a jar full of marbles that had been turned over, but she was sweet natured and didn't sound bothered by his unannounced visit.

"Thank you, Mrs. Bromley."

He reached for the handle at the same time she did. The stubborn rusty hinges screeched as Doug helped her with the door.

"I need to lubricate those darn things," Esther said.

"Oh, I have some lube at home," Doug said. "I'll come over later and apply some. Should take care of that squeal."

"Oh, you're a doll," she said, waving her right hand toward him. She shuffled back to her recliner and gestured toward the sofa with her cane. "Have a seat, darling. I'm just catching an afternoon program." She backed toward the chair, letting her backside fall slowly until she let herself completely collapse into it.

Doug stopped in the doorway. "Oh, would you like me to come back, then?"

"Nope, it's okay." She reached for the remote on the arm of the chair. "I've got that DVR thingy with my cable."

She pressed a few buttons on the remote and turned back to Doug. "I can just pick it up afterward."

"Well, thanks Mrs. Bromley."

"You're so polite," she said, settling into the recliner and resting the cane against the side. "But you can call me Esther, dear."

"Thank you, Esther."

Doug sat back in the olive green corduroy sofa. It didn't have one of those plastic covers one might normally expect to see in an older person's home. She'd once told Doug she didn't believe in "artificial tapestries." She was proud of all her possessions, what few she had, and didn't think it was right to cover them.

He looked past her to the opposite wall and saw a framed photo of what appeared to be a much younger Esther Bromley and her late husband, Warren.

"I'm telling you," Doug said, "that Warren was a lucky man. You were a sexy lady."

Doug's comment had caught her off guard, and when she laughed she coughed a bit, perhaps having inhaled a little saliva.

"You are too much, Doug Mitchell," she said, fanning her face with her right hand. Even through the wrinkles and liver spots, Doug saw her face flush.

"Hey, it's true," he winked.

Esther finished laughing with an "ah," and Doug decided it was a good time to ask her about his property.

"Esther, do you remember who lived on my property before Carla and I got here?"

She stared at him a moment before responding. "Why do you ask?"

"Just curious," he said.

Esther took a deep breath and settled even deeper into the recliner. "Well, it was a long time ago, dear. That house burned down at least ten years before you moved in—maybe more."

"Right, but there had to be *someone* who lived there. I mean, I know there was a foundation there before mine was set. Must have been a house there at one time?"

"Well, sure, there was a house. Why?"

Doug ignored the question. "Do you remember what kind of people they were?"

Her face appeared baffled by what reason Doug would have for asking these questions, but she answered him, anyway. "They were very nice. Few kids—all grown up now, of course."

Doug nodded intently and leaned forward. "Were they spiritual people? Like, did they worship God or...*gods*, or anything like that?"

Esther stared at him. She looked confused at first, but then her eyes narrowed and her head tilted curiously.

"You've never asked me about this before." A slight pause. "Why now?"

Doug finally sat back on the sofa and laughed off the notion of an ulterior motive. "I know," he said. "I'm just curious about the land."

She nodded in reply, but offered no other response. Her eyes remained suspicious.

"Esther," he continued, "does the name 'Achak' mean anything to you?"

Her eyebrows raced up her forehead. "I...I don't recall if I've ever heard that name before."

"Never before?" Doug pressed.

Esther looked away from Doug and squinted her eyes as if trying to look into a locked memory buried somewhere deep in her past. When she was done looking, she said, "No, that name doesn't ring a bell at all."

"Could the man who lived at my property before have been named that?"

Her face now appeared taken aback, even a bit insulted.

"Douglas, I remember very well who used to live there and I'm sure none of them were called such a name. Why wouldn't you just ask me who they were? And who's this Achak person?"

Doug immediately felt the momentum shift and he was now playing defense.

"Uh, ya know, I was just curious. Heard the name somewhere...thought you might have known who it was."

"Uh huh," she said. "And just who *is* this Achak? Do *you* know who he was?"

"You know what," Doug said matter-of-factly, "I probably heard it in the grocery store or something. So how are you? Winter hasn't been too bad for you, I hope?"

A wry smile fell over Esther's lips and she said, "You're lying, Doug, and we both know it."

"What do you mean, Esther?" he asked, pretending to have no idea what she was talking about.

"You've got something in that house of yours, don't you? Something...you don't quite understand or know how to explain?"

Doug pursed his lips, fought for a rebuttal, but it was useless. He exhaled and let his head hang. "Am I that obvious?"

Esther smiled. "It's okay, I don't mind talking about her."

Doug quickly picked up his head. "Her?"

She tented her fingers and exhaled softly, as if she was about to regale him of a decades-old legend. "The woman who lived next door; her name was Vera."

"Woman?" Doug asked. "I thought you said there was a couple?"

Esther smiled. "I'll get to them, I promise."

"Sure. Sorry." Doug leaned forward, put his hands together and rested them on his knees.

"Vera and her first husband, Edgar, were missionaries. They did a lot of work out in Sumatra. When Warren and I moved in, she'd already been living there for about two years. That was in 1953. She had three children, all of whom are still alive, I believe, but they all moved on to Florida, Colorado…and I think the third is out in Cape Cod."

"What did they do in Sumatra?" Doug asked.

"They built churches, taught about God…they mostly worked with the children. Tried to educate them on religion."

"They taught about God? As in the Bible? Do they practice Christianity in Sumatra?"

Esther laughed. "You'll have to forgive me, Doug, I'm an old woman. I don't recall how many different religions are practiced over there. But yes, I believe they were trying to spread the word of God."

Doug bowed his head, apologetically. "Of course. Sorry. Please, go on."

"Well, unfortunately, her husband was murdered by some people who didn't agree with what she and Edgar were preaching."

"Terrorists?" Doug said.

Esther nodded. "Vera was completely lost after that. Aside from the work they did, he was her entire life. She tried to continue her missionary work, but before long, she got very lonely and moved back to the U.S. It took a long time, but years later she married a man and they had three wonderful children."

"Is the husband still around?" Doug asked.

Esther's expression turned grim. "They both perished in the fire that destroyed the house."

"Oh, wow. So they died inside as the house burned down around them?"

Esther nodded slowly.

"They didn't try to escape?"

She shrugged. "Maybe they did. I never found out. All the police determined was that they died of asphyxiation. They were badly burned, as you can imagine, but it's likely that they died before the flames got to them."

A horrifying image played inside Doug's head. "That's awful."

"Sorry, dear, I didn't mean to appall you."

Doug looked up. "Oh, no, not at all. It's just sad. Terrible, really."

They sat in silence for a while with Doug absorbing the details of the story and Esther allowing him to do so.

After a minute, Doug said, "The kids had already moved out then, I assume?"

"Oh, the kids were fine. They were already married and starting families of their own. Didn't make it any easier, of course."

"Oh, no, I wouldn't expect it to be."

Esther looked off, her eyes seeing something that wasn't in the room. A past memory, Doug assumed.

"What is it?" he asked.

"She wrote a book about him," she said. "About Edgar."

Doug was happy to engage in a lighter topic. "Really? Like a biography or something?"

"She loved that man with all her heart and wrote about the things he did—how he helped people in countries like Sumatra."

"What is it called?"

"The book was called, *O Bok Su*. I'm not sure what it means, but I remember the title because it sounded so different from any other book I'd ever heard of."

Doug thought he'd finally made a discovery. "So you think the book explains what's going on in my house?"

"I've never read it," she said bluntly.

"Oh," Doug said.

"But they say spirits of people who die very tragic and unexpected deaths sometimes have trouble…um…finding the light, I guess." She struggled to find a better explanation. "Finding their way home, maybe."

"Finding heaven?" Doug offered.

She raised a crooked finger and pointed at him. "That's it. Finding heaven."

"Hm," Doug thought. He wasn't a very religious man, but he was raised Catholic and still mildly aware of the doctrine. "I suppose entry into heaven depends on what you did in life, right?"

Esther's eyes became intense and her face deadpan. "Vera was a very spiritual person, Doug. As long as I knew her, she never did wrong in her life and she gave more than she received."

Doug dropped his head and nodded, regretful that he'd soured Vera's memory in any way.

"I know she meditated a lot," Esther continued. "And while she'd probably never admit it to her second husband, she often tried to communicate with Edgar. Through meditation."

"Really?"

Esther nodded quietly.

"Was she ever successful?"

"Depends on what you consider success," she said. "Successful in speaking with Edgar? I can't say for sure. But…successful in speaking with other spirits? Oh, I'm pretty sure she found what she needed through her meditation."

"You seem confident about that," Doug said. "How come? If you don't mind my asking."

"Of course I don't. I'm confident because I helped her communicate with several of them."

Doug felt a tingle sweep across the back of his neck and upper shoulders.

"You did?"

"Mm-hmm. Vera was a very special person, Doug."

Doug smiled and didn't speak. He wanted to give Esther as much room as she needed to continue.

"Vera asked me to join her during several of her sessions. She knew I was also a woman of faith and told me that, together, we could combine our energies, which would help us communicate with the spirits."

"Who did you talk to?" Doug asked intently.

"Oh, I never spoke to anybody."

Doug's face dropped in mild disappointment.

"But Vera..." Esther continued. "She talked to many."

"Do you remember any of them? Any of their names?"

Esther shook her head. "It was a long time ago."

Doug nodded. "I understand."

He sat and waited. He couldn't think of any other questions to ask and it seemed as if Esther had told him everything she could remember. There was no sense in waiting to see if any other inquiries would manifest in his head. He stood up to leave.

Those Among Us

"Well, thank you for the chat, Esther. I appreciate it."

He reached and took her hand while she sat in the chair. She smiled up at him.

"You're most welcome, Doug."

"I'll let you get back to your show. Oh, and I'll come by later and fix that door."

"You're too sweet, dear."

"Nah, it's my pleasure."

Doug let go of her hand and walked out of the living room toward the front door. As he turned the handle, Esther leaned forward in her chair.

"You know," she said, "it wouldn't surprise me if some of those spirits she talked to are still on your property."

Doug froze at the door and didn't turn around.

"Maybe even that Achak man is one of them," she said.

CHAPTER 16

Doug left Esther's house, walked down the deteriorated stairs, passed the pots holding dead flower roots, and onto the short stone walkway in front of her home. He'd hoped to feel lighter, like a weight had been lifted. He had expected to feel as if a burden had been removed from his subconscious, that there was an explanation for all of this, but instead of answers he was left only with additional questions.

He found his home empty when he entered. He wasn't sure how long he'd been gone. There was a note on the edge of the breakfast bar that read: "Took Janie to my parents' house. Be back in a little while. Or, come and join us."

Doug removed a beer from the fridge and sat at the table in the kitchen. He pondered quietly as he sipped and stared at nothing, his eyes blurring as his thoughts took over.

Maybe I'm going about this all wrong. Whatever is here obviously wants to communicate. It just doesn't want to communicate with me.

He thought about the voice recorder sitting in the top drawer of his desk and about what other strategies he could try.

He sat up straight and looked around as a sudden realization came over him.

"Maybe I don't have to be sneaky around *it*," he said aloud. He took another sip, swallowed and asked, "Do you want to talk to me?"

No answer.

Then an idea seeded itself into his brain and quickly bloomed into something with plausibility. He took one more sip, stood from the table, and headed for the study. He felt a renewed determination to find answers, to try to communicate with whatever was making its home in Janie's bedroom. He crossed the threshold between the kitchen and the hallway, passed Janie's bedroom—

What was that?

He stopped in the hallway. From the edge of his vision, barely visible on the fringe, there had been a woman. He felt the small hairs on his arms raise and curl over as they pressed against the inside of his sweater.

Did I just see that?

The image began to manifest in the eye of his mind, began to take shape. A woman had been sitting on the bed. On Janie's bed.

She'd looked at him.

Doug stood in the hallway, unsure whether to turn and look into Janie's room or turn and run out of the house. His heart now raced, but he breathed slowly and with control.

I have to see.

He relaxed his hands, realizing he'd been clenching them into fists, and turned around. As he walked back toward Janie's room, the image became clearer in his mind: Blue shirt, collared. Long sleeves. Long, black hair. Black pants. Conservative-looking shoes.

And were those feathers on her pants?

As he reached the doorway to her room, he simultaneously hoped the woman was gone, but also that he would see her. He turned the corner.

The room was empty. He released a long breath, unaware he'd even been holding it. His eyes quickly and thoroughly scanned the entire visible space of her room. There was nobody.

Then, as his eyes adjusted to the surroundings, he noticed something different. Doug looked at the bed, at where he'd seen the image of the woman sitting. The edge of the mattress was indented.

The hell?

He cautiously walked over to the bed to get a closer look. Perhaps his eyes had tricked him from this distance? Granted, it was only several feet from the door, but still...

As he closed the space between him and the bed, the air began to thicken, as if walking through a dry fog.

Three feet.

Doug looked up, peeled his eyelids wide, and tried to erase any lingering "floaters" from his vision.

Two feet.

The air had grown incredibly dense and it was difficult to breathe deeply. Doug blinked rapidly and then shut his eyes tightly, pressing his lids together until he saw bright lights at the center. He opened them and blinked rapidly again. He rubbed his eyes with his fists.

One foot.

He looked straight ahead at the wall. His sight adjusted and he looked down.

A slight depression in the comforter.

Doug rubbed his eyes some more, blinked again, and then stared at the comforter.

The curvature remained—a concavity, as if an invisible sphere sat on the edge of the bed. And then, gently, the comforter released, the curve disappeared, and the fabric returned to its usual flat position.

Doug's feet froze to the floor. Even if he wanted to jump or step backward, it would have been impossible. For the moment, his brain was incapable of sending messages to his extremities; it was trying to assimilate what his eyes had just seen and contrast that information with everything else Doug knew about the natural world.

A sudden displacement of air. A slight breeze floated through the closely cut hair near his temple. His body swayed as the presence of another being passed by him. Or through him. He didn't know anymore. In that moment, he didn't even care to try to understand.

He thought about asking a question, but the combination of his breath having caught in his chest and the idea that he might actually *receive* an answer both prevented and frightened him from doing so. This wasn't a time for verbal communication. For if it had been, he was sure that whatever (or *whoever*) was in the room with him would have made some kind of verbal announcement. As it was, he was certain his present company was communicating plenty. The message was loud and clear.

I am here.

A song began to play to Doug's left and he recognized it at once: Janie's snow globe had mysteriously found its maestro. Quite past the point of shock, Doug steered his head left toward the shelf. Having apparently wound itself, the snow globe played its sweet melody. *Let It Snow* chimed as metal pins plucked away at the lamellae, and Doug's mind waded farther out into the vast new ocean of possibility and lingered until another unexplained phenomenon floated along.

After a full chorus, the snow globe stopped.

Five seconds later, the air felt thinner…lighter.

Ten seconds later, Doug left Janie's room.

CHAPTER 17

Saturday afternoon progressed much the same as a typical school day; Carla returned from her parents' and Janie immediately went to her room and closed the blinds and door. She stayed there for several hours talking and playing...but mostly talking.

Doug told Carla about his visit with Esther and about his "encounter" in Janie's room. Carla remained skeptical.

"Are you sure you're not doing this to yourself?" she asked. "Maybe you stepped on the carpet and you hit a weak board or something and it shook the wall."

Doug stared at her blankly. "Really? I stepped on a board? I shook a *wall*?" he spread his arms out. "And a damn snow globe turned itself on?"

Carla didn't look at him and only continued to stand in front of the kitchen stove, occasionally stirring battered chicken and vegetables with a wooden spoon in a large skillet.

"How do I manage to shake a goddamn wall, with my looks?" he persisted.

Carla snapped the spoon on the top of the stove and shot daggers into his eyes. "I don't know, Doug," she hissed. "You're obsessed with this shit lately and frankly, I'm getting tired of it."

Doug's eyes widened. "You're what? You're *getting tired*?"

Carla broke his stare and grabbed the spoon. She continued to stir the food.

Doug continued, "Guess what hon'? I've been tired since Thanksgiving! It's every day and night now with this shit. Janie can't get it together in school long enough to keep the teacher from thinking she's fucked up. Meanwhile, when's the last time the three of us sat down and had dinner as a family?"

Carla sighed. She rested the spoon on the stove more gently this time. "Doug, I'm exhausted. I really am."

Doug turned away and rubbed his palm against his forehead.

"I'm exhausted from talking about this," Carla continued. "We don't talk about anything else anymore. It's always, 'what did Janie do today?' 'Did she go straight to her room again?' 'Did you hear anything last night?' 'What if we try doing some EVPs?'" She paused for a moment. "I still think it's a phase."

Doug scoffed as he paced in the kitchen.

I can't believe she still thinks it's a fucking phase.

He wasn't winning any arguments tonight. Sadly, neither was Carla and Doug knew it, which was worse because when there's *no* winner, there's also no loser. And in these situations, both parties can claim victory, and both did.

Doug stopped pacing and looked at her. "Well," he said. "We'll see what the *phase* has to say."

Carla shook her head. "What the hell does that mean?"

"Before you guys got home, I put the voice recorder in her room and hit record—just as you both walked in the door."

As Doug slept, he dreamt of his earlier experience in Janie's room. He watched the dream in third person, staring over his shoulder and never seeing his own face. The only thing different in the dream was that Janie was there...talking to her "friend."

"This is my daddy," she said, staring up into thin air at what would be about eye-height for an average adult. "He's saying 'hi,'" Janie said to Doug, but he couldn't hear her friend.

"Hi," Doug said, and weakly waved his hand.

"Mr. Achak wants to know if he can stay here, Daddy. Pleeease! Can he stay?"

"Oh, all right," Doug heard himself saying.

Janie reached out and hugged him tightly. "Now we can all play together," she said. "Here, Daddy, Mr. Achak is trying to give you something."

Doug looked in the direction of where he assumed Mr. Achak to be. There was nothing. He saw straight through to the window, the walls, and her dresser. It was empty space. An eerie void filled only with the vivid imagination of a seven-year-old.

"Take it, Daddy," Janie said.

As Doug stared out, a form began to take shape. To his surprise, it looked rather human. He could see the outline of a head, some shoulders, and the upper torso. But he could not see any features, only a black mass shaped like a person. Then the mass leaned forward into Doug.

"Isn't it nice, Daddy?" Janie asked.

Doug could no longer speak. The darkened shape closed in on him and he couldn't move at all. Even with no features and no way of expressing emotion, the shape felt ominous, threatening, and Doug instinctively backed away. He moved just in time to see Janie's door close behind him. He reached for the handle, turned, and looked over his shoulder as he twisted the knob back and forth. The dark mass kept coming. Doug worked the door handle over and over, but it wouldn't budge. He stopped and turned again. The mass was only inches away from him. If it were a live person, they would have been toe to toe.

"Take it, Daddy, take it!"

Doug was confused. He saw nothing to take and no hands to take from.

"Take it, Daddy!" Janie laughed.

His daughter's urging was sincere and harmless, but the mass was anything but. And although he could not see what it was the thing wanted to give him, Doug knew he didn't want it.

The dark mass was now on him. In him. Occupying his space. Doug felt needles digging out from under his skin. He turned to Janie.

"What is this?" he asked.

"He's *you*, Daddy."

Doug woke up. He pulled the sheets down to examine his body. He patted his chest, shoulders and arms. It was just him. No dark mass filled him or presented itself to him. He turned and saw Carla sleeping peacefully. He then rested his head on the pillow, taking deep but silent breaths so as not to wake her.

"*Ahhh*"

Doug felt a warm breeze against his face.

Was that me?

He listened. He heard nothing but the swirling winter wind pawing at their windows, trying to invade their heated haven.

Then he felt the breeze again.

"Ahhh"

Doug's eyes widened as there was no mistaking the sound of the breath that fell over his face. He could even feel the slightest edge of a lip against his skin.

He turned toward the source of the breathing and sank into his pillow. Another warm breath of air wafted across his eyes. He heard the breathing, intense and primal; the way a wild animal might do after it's killed its prey. Yet, there was nobody there, nobody he could see. Only the dark still emptiness of their bedroom.

A sudden jolt kicked the bed to the right. Doug shot up and reached for his wife as he stared at the corner of the mattress.

"Carla?" he said loudly, but she was already awake.

"Doug, what the hell are you doing?"

The bed moved again. This time it lifted from the floor and crashed down, the feet of the bed scuffing against the carpet.

"Doug!" Carla yelled.

Then the bed moved once more. Doug and Carla both shouted for each other as the bed was pushed to the side a couple feet. Carla grabbed at Doug's shirt as she screamed and pulled the sheets up to her face. Doug held her with both hands, shouting nothing that made any sense.

Then the bed stopped.

Footsteps pounded on the floor a second later, leading from the foot of the bed, to the door and into the hallway. They didn't stop as they shot down the hall and, by Doug's estimation, into the kitchen. After that, the footsteps disappeared.

"Where did it go?" Carla asked.

Doug tilted his head upward, his fingertips curled slightly into the bed sheet. "I don't know," he whispered. "Seems like it stopped when it reached the kitchen."

"So it's just standing in the kitchen?" she asked.

"Shit," Doug thought out loud. "I don't know. That doesn't make any sense."

A dull *tap-tap-tap* raced across the floor. The footsteps had changed direction and headed back toward the bedrooms. Then they stopped, some distance from Doug and Carla's room. Closer to Janie's room.

Doug quietly breathed in short, quick breaths. He ignored the pinching of Carla's fingers as she dug her grip into his arm. He slowly began to slide a leg toward the edge of the bed, the sheets quiet and forgiving of the movement.

"Mommy?" said a small voice immediately identifiable as Janie's. She sounded confused.

Doug had one leg over the edge of the bed and quickly began sliding the other one.

"*Mommy!*"

Doug and Carla jumped from the mattress. The handle of the door crashed against the wall as Doug swung it open and bounded into the hall; the several feet that separated their two rooms felt like a mile.

Janie screamed again and Doug's only wish was that her room was just a few inches closer to his—just one or two fewer steps he'd have to make before he could reach her. The raw, sick, helpless feeling that comes with being a father at the time his child needs him most and he just can't seem to get to her fast enough was a harsh, spiteful kick to Doug's heart.

Doug reached her door and it required some effort to push it open, as if a large, heavy object stood on the other side, not quite forcing the door closed, but not simply allowing entry either. A wall of cold stopped Doug as he finally made enough space to move into the room.

"Holy shit," he said. "It's freezing in here." One hand wrapped around the opposite arm as the other flicked on the light switch. He and Carla hurried to Janie's bed, both of them sitting on opposite sides of their daughter.

Janie's eyes wandered the room. There was white panic on her forehead and cheeks. Doug noticed vapor escaping from her mouth as she exhaled. Doug unconsciously pursed his own lips and did the same; he watched as his breath fogged and dissipated.

"Jesus," Carla said, her arms wrapped around Janie. "She's freezing, Doug. Touch her skin."

Doug rested his hand on Janie's arm. The chill was immediate upon touching her, and her tiny chest heaved in and out as she shivered both from the cold air and the fierce awakening. Doug looked around the room — for what he wasn't sure — but Janie seemed to be searching for something, and he tried to follow her actions in the event she saw something.

"Wanna tell us what happened?" Carla asked her.

Janie took a few shallow breaths before she started crying, "I can't sleep with all the lights in my room!" She hugged Carla tighter.

Carla shot a look at Doug and mouthed, *"What?"*

Doug remained silent and only shrugged. He stood and began pacing the room, trying to think of possible explanations. He walked to Janie's window and pulled back the curtain. Perhaps a car had been parked with its headlights on and shone in Janie's window. But he saw no cars. None of the neighbors' houses even had their exterior lights on, and their home was far enough from the road to rule out traffic as a cause of the disturbance.

"What lights are you talking about, J-Bird?" he asked.

"The lights in my room!" Janie cried again.

"Okay," Carla said, holding her closer. "Shh, it's okay. We're all here now. The lights can't hurt you." She glanced at Doug again, who was shaking his head without any logical explanation.

"Where were the lights coming from, Sweetie?" he asked.

"They were everywhere!" Janie's breathing had slowed and the tears weren't as many as they were a few moments ago.

Doug stepped closer and crouched into a catcher's position in front of her. He took her hand.

"What did they look like, Sweetie?"

Janie unburied her face from Carla's shoulder and wiped a hand across her eyes. "They looked like little circles. They were flying around my room. I heard someone walking around out in the hall and I thought it was you."

The look Doug hurled at Carla conveyed only one meaning:

I told you so.

Carla grudgingly nodded in accordance.

Before either Doug or Carla could respond, Janie asked, "Can I sleep in your bed tonight?"

"Sure, baby," Carla said. She stood and took Janie by the hand and they walked out of the room.

Doug looked around, expecting to see the entity show itself like it had earlier in the day, but it stayed hidden behind the doors and walls of the natural world.

But he knew it was there. He could feel it watching him as he paced around the room and even as he left. He knew because he felt the same heaviness he'd experienced when he last planted the voice recorder. And for the first time since the events began, Doug was angry.

The feeling he experienced as he left Janie's room was one of being forced out, as if an unseen hand had pushed him away. He didn't like that feeling. It pissed him off. He now felt a genuine anger toward the entity—much like one feels after he/she has been cheaply bested by a rival.

What scared him was the idea that this being likely didn't care how Doug felt. And after her reaction to the "lights" in her room, Mr. Achak likely didn't care how Janie felt, either.

That kept Doug awake and alert until the sun flooded his room in the morning. And long after Janie and Carla had gotten out of bed.

CHAPTER 18

It was Sunday. The irony that it was the Lord's Day was not lost on Doug as he sat alone in his study, slouching in his leather swivel desk chair, listening to playback from the voice recorder and hoping to hear the voice of a spirit.

The open design of his supra-aural headphones could at times be a disadvantage since sound could easily leak out. The advantage, however, was that he would be able to hear most external sounds should anyone call for him. Or if anyone should barge through the door and try to catch him unawares.

As a measure of privacy, Doug had the foresight to lock the door. Twice already he'd heard the door handle jiggle—someone's not-so-subtle attempt to gain entry into the room.

Doug stared at the data on the voice recorder:

File A – 2:06.

The first file had recorded a little over two hours of sound. Doug had hidden the recorder behind the TV/DVD combo that sat on Janie's dresser in front of the bed. Either she'd never noticed it, or nobody had shown her where to look. Or both.

Having no other files on the recorder, Doug pressed the circular button at the center of the device and the file began to play.

The recording was soft, barely audible. He thumbed around and found two arrow buttons—the volume controls. As he pressed the Up arrow, a meter appeared in the corner of the small square screen. The meter barely registered. Doug continued pressing the arrow and he watched the meter grow as the sound filled his headphones. Janie was talking to her dolls.

"And now it's time to get dressed," she said. "We have school and we don't want to be late."

The sound was amazingly bright and clear. Doug noticed a slight hiss that came with the increase in volume— "white noise"—but it hardly affected the clarity of the recording.

There were other noises that accompanied her voice, everything from shuffling to sliding to sniffling. The recorder's microphone was so sensitive that Doug heard Janie's hand brush and push off against the mattress several times. He could even hear her chapped, weather-cracked hands on the Berber carpet as skin thorns plucked at the fabric.

Then he heard whispers. Not Janie's voice. Janie was still talking, and yet, there was another voice underneath and around Janie's pantomiming.

Doug straightened in his chair, found the Rewind button on the recorder, and backed it up several seconds. He raised the volume meter again before pressing Play. The ambient noise was much louder now, but so was Janie's speech, and he could still hear her as clear as though she sat right next to him.

The whispers were louder, too. There were several of them, but Doug still couldn't make out what they were saying. He backed up the recording once more and wrapped his hands around the ear cups as he listened. First he heard Janie:

"Mommy's gonna make supper soon, so we have to wash our hands."

Then, just under her voice, Doug heard a whisper:

"Maybe we should leave..."

Leave? Doug thought. He didn't understand what it meant and kept listening.

Janie: "I hope she makes pancakes...ha ha ha! That would be silly: pancakes for supper!"

Inaudible whisper.

Across the room, Doug saw the door handle turn slightly, impeded only by the lock. The handle wiggled once more and then it stopped.

Doug backed up the recording again. He pushed Play and inhaled deeply, waited for Janie to finish speaking, and then concentrated on the second voice:

"I don't like this place."

He continued listening to the interaction between Janie and her...visitor. There was a long period where only Janie spoke. At times Doug was unable to tell whether she was speaking directly to the entity itself or to her dolls. He supposed it could have been both.

At the thirty-two minute mark, the visitor announced itself again. This time, the whispered voice immediately followed Janie's voice. And it was at once identifiable.

Janie: "And I told you...you have to stop doing that, but you don't listen."

Voice: *"...these fucking people!"*

Doug stopped the recording. The words echoed in his head.

These fucking people.

The gravelly-voiced and whispered words continued to repeat themselves and he stared at the tiny machine as if it were some foreign, alien technology not from this earth. He turned the device in his hand, half-expecting to see a voice recorder-sized demon clinging to the back, but there was nothing.

These fucking people.

The door handle wiggled again. This time, there was more force behind the jarring motion. No voice though. Nobody asking for him or calling his name. Only a silent, would-be intruder. Doug was sure it was Janie. Something or somebody had likely advised her that he was listening to a recording of a recent play session and instructed her to stop it.

Doug's thoughts swirled feverishly.

What about these fucking people? Are you happy *with these fucking people? Are you* angry *with these fucking people?*

He thought about the nature of Janie's conversation. Over the last thirty-plus minutes she hadn't shown any fear or hesitation toward whatever was in her room. Her tone was candid and playful. Doug assumed this was a good sign and considered the entity was only acting similarly, in its own way. Clearly, it was an adult presence.

After several minutes of hesitation and second-guessing, Doug pressed Play.

Janie's voice again came on, just as pleasant and mellifluous as it did before. He didn't even pay attention to her anymore. He was listening to the void before, after, and in between her words. The white noise—the sound that occurred in the emptiness of space, fueled by the spirit of another.

When the voice spoke again, the message was clear:

"The people must go."

The door handle wiggled once more. Doug backed up the recording and played it again. He had to confirm exactly what he'd heard.

It was no different the second time around.

"The people must go."

The door handle wiggled again. Hard.

Doug stopped the recorder. He pulled off the headphones, opened the middle drawer of his desk, and shoved the device and the headphones inside. He took a key from the top of the desk, locked the drawer, and shoved the key in his pocket.

The door handle turned vigorously.

Doug stood from his desk, walked around it, and then opened the door.

Janie stood there. Her eyes narrowed, questioning her father's activity. Doug felt her eyes trying desperately to read him, but he wasn't going to give away anything today.

"What are you doing, Daddy?"

"I was uh...doing some work, J-Bird." He stared at her eyes, relaxed all the muscles in his face. Hers was taut, fierce. Before she had a chance to question him again, he called an offensive play. "What are *you* doing, Janie?"

She looked at him, her head tilted. Doug could tell she knew something was amiss, but she didn't have enough ammunition to fire back, not like she did the other day.

After a few seconds of silence, she said, "Mommy said to say it's time for supper."

"Okay, J-Bird, sounds good."

Doug stood in the doorway, Janie opposite him. She looked past him into the study. She looked left toward the bookcase, then right, toward his glass cabinet of sports memorabilia. She was trying to find something, anything she could use.

Doug stood his ground and waited for her to leave. When she wouldn't stop looking, he asked, "What is mommy making?"

Janie's eyes stuttered before finally resting on his. "I don't know," she said stubbornly. "Something with chicken."

"Mmm," Doug said with a smile. "Sounds good."

Janie didn't smile back, her intense expression lingering before she finally walked away toward the kitchen.

Doug followed and pulled the door closed behind him.

CHAPTER 19

"The *fucking* people?" Carla blurted out.

Long after Janie had gone to sleep, when Doug was certain she was unconscious, he removed the voice recorder from the top drawer of his desk and brought it into the bedroom so Carla could listen to the recordings. He'd marked on a sheet of paper the precise time of each of the mystery voice's appearances so it would be simple to queue each sound and get Carla's opinion.

She found the first two EVPs curious, but ultimately harmless, just as Doug had. However, she reacted to the third exactly how Doug had expected.

"Shh!" he pleaded after she had shrieked. He ticked his head back quickly toward the hallway. "I don't want her to hear us listening to this."

Carla pulled the headphones away from her ears and asked in a lowered voice, "You really think she'd know what this is?"

Doug's face was stern. "I do."

Carla's eyes questioned him, but she said nothing.

"She's been in my face about this stuff lately," Doug continued. He went on to tell Carla about the day Janie had interrogated him about being in her room, and about the way she'd continuously tried to open the door to the study when he was reviewing the recordings.

"Yeah, but I told her to go tell you dinner was ready," Carla said.

"Okay, then what was up with her questioning me like a murder suspect?"

Carla's eyes widened, but she shook her head. "Well...honestly, I don't know. That is kinda strange."

"Damn right it is."

They sat and stared at each other a few moments until Carla's gaze wandered slightly, looked around briefly, then returned to Doug.

"Play it again."

As Carla stretched the headphones over her ears, Doug backed up the last EVP and pushed Play. He watched Carla listen with her ears as well as her eyes; they darted around the room with concentration. Then they remained still. And wide. Doug stopped the device and Carla took off the headphones. Her eyes again wandered, listlessly, as she searched for a logical explanation that would remain unformed.

When it appeared by her expression she had finally accepted what her ears told her as truth, she asked, "You said there's one more?"

Doug nodded.

"Okay," she said. "Let me hear it."

Doug consulted the small sheet of paper and pushed the Fast-Forward button on the recorder, advancing the recording several minutes before stopping.

"Okay," he said as Carla moved the headphones over her ears once again. "This one is pretty obvious. You shouldn't have any trouble hearing what's being said."

He pushed Play again and studied Carla's face. He watched as she showed both intrigue and patience. She leaned forward slightly, straining to hear every word, every sound, as clearly as possible. Her fingers knotted in her lap.

Then Doug saw curiosity switch over to panic, and then fear. The muscles in her face tightened; she reached up and nervously scratched her shoulder. Both hands moved toward the headphones, but she hesitated, unable to decide whether or not to take them off. Doug could see she was fighting despair. Until now, Carla had considered the occurrences in the house only to be harmless coincidences. Although she afforded Doug the freedom to carry on with his talk of spirits and haunts, she'd merely joked about it, never once actually believing in the possibility of such things. But as Doug stared into her face, he saw defeat. Sadness. Humiliation. Most of all, he saw acceptance.

Carla sat still, her eyes glossed over, her hands once again in her lap, open and empty. Doug motioned toward the headphones. Carla blinked slowly and nodded. He pulled each of the cups away from her ears, lifted the headband off her hair, and set them down on the bed. Carla's eyes did not meet his and they filled with tears. Instead of wiping them away, she let them fall unevenly over her freckled cheeks and over her lips.

Doug sat quietly and waited for her to say something. When she did, he was happy he wasn't the one to break the silence.

"So, what do we do now?" she asked.

"I think I'm going to talk to a priest. Maybe someone can come bless the house."

"But we're not religious people," she said.

He shrugged. "I don't know what else to do." He allowed a few moments to pass and waited for her to interject. When it was apparent she had no further rebuttal, he said, "There's something in the house, Carla. Possibly some*one*. I don't know how to deal with this. I'm just going with my gut here."

He was caught completely off-guard when she threw her arms around him. She leaned into him and he tightened his core to keep from falling backward and off the bed.

"Oh my god, Doug, our baby!" Carla said. Doug heard her voice break and felt her chest shudder against his as the sobs crashed forth like waves at high tide. "It's in her room!"

"I know," he said calmly. "I know." He pulled her close and stroked her back with one hand. "We're going to find out what's going on, I promise."

"Okay," she said weakly.

"Okay?" he urged.

She sniffled, took a deep breath. "Okay." There was a bit more resolve in her voice this time, but she was still distressed. It would take more than his own reassurance, Doug realized, for Carla to fully believe and have faith in their course. They would need someone who understood this.

In all the years they'd been together, through dating and then marriage, Doug had only seen Carla cry once before. That was when Janie was born. They were tears of joy then, spawned from the promise of innocence and new life; a new beginning. Now she cried out of fear. Fear of the unknown, of the danger that potentially surrounded her family, and of the damage that might have already been done.

For the second time, she cried for Janie.

CHAPTER 20

In the week that followed, activity in the home increased exponentially. It was as if the intensity and frequency of the activity was in direct response to the Mitchells' collective awareness, their acceptance of, and response to, what was happening.

Carla, once the skeptic, had finally succumbed to the realization the entity was real, and that what she had previously interpreted as "coincidences" were in fact some kind of spiritual manifestations. The TV turning itself on and off as she oversaw the daycare children was no longer electrical interference, static, or otherwise. Wine glasses that fell and broke inside their hutch didn't do so as a result of a walk-by vibration. Window drafts weren't the cause of doors opening and shutting violently by themselves. In fact, the latter was staunchly confirmed by Janie.

During lunch one day, as Carla and the daycare children sat in the kitchen eating macaroni and cheese, the cellar door had suddenly unlatched itself, opened, and quickly banged into the sidewall. The children all jumped in their highchairs and looked to see who had caused the disturbance. Even Carla, having grown somewhat accustomed to happenings of this nature, shook in her seat as the door *chonged* open. The door swung back slowly from the wall and remained open for several seconds before another impetus drove it back into its frame, latching it forcefully. The sound echoed with a rush throughout the house and then fell silent once again. The children all turned to Carla for…protection? Consolation? They each looked to her for words that would explain what had just happened. Carla knew it was only the ghost's way of telling her it was there.

Watching.

Waiting.

She reached into the darkened closet of her mind for reasons that might make sense to a bunch of toddlers, but in the end it was not her reason to give.

Janie, who'd been enjoying lunch with the daycare after a half-day at school, calmly explained, "It's just the ghost, guys. Sheesh."

Several days later, as another work day wound down and parents arrived to pick up their children, Carla observed three-year-old Nicholas Thompson's mother, Margaret, looking curiously around the house as she stood in the foyer waiting for her son to gather his things.

Carla watched as Margaret's eyes appeared to study certain aspects of the home. Perhaps she'd been following a dust bunny floating through the air.

Perhaps it was something else.

As they both waited for little Nicholas to procure his coat from the closet in the hallway, Carla asked, "Is there a bug in here?" Her tone was purposely innocuous and inoffensive.

Margaret jerked her head toward Carla, seemingly startled by the question. "Oh, no. I was just looking around. You have a very nice house."

"Well, thank you," Carla said. "It's one of the newer homes on the street."

Margaret nodded, her eyes again drifting away...up...down.

"We like to paint every once in a while, too...to keep it fresh," Carla continued, all the while eyeing Margaret's disengaged expression. "One day, we'd like to turn it into a truck stop."

Margaret twisted her head toward Carla, eyes narrowed and lines of confusion drawn between her brows. Carla simply stared back at the mother, her expression flat, awaiting a response. She'd baited Margaret well and it would only be a matter of seconds until Margaret knew she'd been made.

Carla watched as Margaret's eyes eventually relaxed and her face drooped of embarrassment.

"I'm sorry," she said.

"It's okay," Carla accepted. "Anything you want to ask me?"

Margaret sighed and her eyes lowered. Then, as she looked up at Carla again, a wry smile began to form on her lips. "You guys have ghosts in here?"

"Only one ghost," Carla said flatly.

Margaret tried to hide the surprise, but Carla caught it; Margaret's eyelids fluttered and her nostrils flared just briefly.

"Oh," Margaret said with a mock laugh. "Just one?"

"Yep," Carla spoke confidently. "We've only been able to confirm one. His name is Mr. Achak and he stays in Janie's room mostly."

Margaret Thompson's face dropped. "You're not kidding?"

"Would you be asking if you thought it wasn't real?" Carla asked. She watched as Margaret's mouth opened and closed, but no words came forth. Her arms, which once hung peacefully at her sides, were now cocked at awkward, uncomfortable angles. Carla remained quiet and waited again for a rehearsed response; she watched as Margaret physically tried to backpedal out of the conversation. When her shoulders slumped and her back rounded casually, Carla knew Margaret had nothing left.

"I'm sorry...again."

Carla nodded, accepting her apology.

"It's just that...Nicholas came home the other day talking about ghosts and how your daughter mentioned something about a ghost in the daycare and I…" She fought for more words, but ultimately gave up.

"It's all right," Carla assured her. "Like I said, the ghost pretty much stays in Janie's room. He never bothers the daycare."

Carla watched as Margaret's expression, once dubious and afraid, now turned studious, hanging on every one of Carla's words.

"There's really nothing to fear here," Carla continued.

"Does Janie feel the same?"

Carla's eyes went north a tick and then settled back on Margaret's. "Janie's fine. She had some difficulty with it at first, as any child would."

Margaret nodded intently.

"But she's fine now. Heck," Carla chuckled, "sometimes she and the ghost play with her dolls."

Margaret laughed an empty, disbelieving laugh.

Just then, Nicholas ran up, his arms tangled in the sleeves of his coat. "Mommy, I can't do it." Margaret squatted and helped Nicholas' arms into his coat and then zipped up the front.

"Well," Margaret started, her eyes darting back and forth as she searched for the right words to say. "Oh, say thank you to Mrs. Mitchell, Nicholas."

"Thank you, Mrs. Mitchell."

Carla patted the top of his moppish brown hair. "You're welcome, Sweetie. I'll see you tomorrow."

"Bye," Margaret said as she walked out the door holding Nicholas' hand.

Carla waved back. When the door closed behind Margaret Thompson and her son, Carla buried her face in her hands and began to sob.

When Carla told Doug about the interaction with Margaret Thompson later that night, Doug felt sick. Though he was the breadwinner of the family, the daycare still equated to a nice chunk of their livelihood. If parents started to believe there was any kind of paranormal activity at the daycare, they might be inclined to pull their kids out in favor of a facility that endorses only *normal* activity. On the other hand, even if the parents didn't believe in such things, they might still leave the daycare if they felt Carla was an unfit caretaker.

"Is she a talker?" Doug asked across the kitchen table. "Will the entire parent base know about this now?"

Carla's shoulders stooped with fragile nerves and exhaustion. She wore distress like a rusted suit of armor and dragged worry around like concrete blocks shackled to her ankles. Doug hated seeing her like that and he secretly wondered if she'd seen *him* the same way in the weeks and months prior—a worn-down, beaten shell of the person he once was. As he watched the tension in her neck and arms grow like fungus, Doug felt it was like looking into a mirror.

"I don't know if she talks to them," she answered. "I hope not."

Even her eyes were heavy with fatigue and anguish.

Doug felt a soft wind push at his back. When he turned, Janie was standing there. She looked tired—arms heavy, head hanging, eyelids puffy and wanting of sleep.

"Hey, J-Bird," Doug said softly. "Can't sleep?"

She shook her head.

"What's the matter?"

"Mr. Achak wants to know when we're leaving."

"Umm…" Doug started. He glanced at Carla and then back to Janie. "I…didn't know we were going anywhere."

"Mr. Achak says he wants us to leave the house. He says it's his home."

The lines in Doug's brow raced up his forehead as that last bit of information bounced around inside his cortex. He'd wondered, more than once, if this moment might someday come. But as many times as he'd thought of it, he hadn't actually prepared himself for it. This was entirely new ground over which he had yet to walk. The entity that lived in the negative space within their home had officially laid down the gauntlet. It was now up to Doug to respond. Janie was far too young to manage this on her own, and Carla was coming unstitched one thread at a time.

The time for discovery and exploration had come and gone. The activity that had simmered for many months had finally reached its boiling point. Within their home, the door between the worlds of the living and the dead had remained shut for many years.

Doug had no idea he was about to reopen it.

CHAPTER 21

Doug spent the first part of Saturday morning placing calls to several area churches to see about having a priest come bless their home. To his chagrin, he was turned down every time. Having not been a member of *any* church—neither he nor Carla—Doug began to wonder if his lack of "practice" in any religion had been detrimental to his pursuit of help. Each time the question, "Are you a member of the church?" had been asked, he'd replied, "No." After that, he'd simply been told, repeatedly, "The church no longer performs blessings of the home."

After the third rejection, Doug knew it was bullshit. He had plenty of friends who'd had their homes blessed over the years. Either he'd just happened to call the only three churches in western Massachusetts that didn't perform blessings, or they had no interest in helping a non-parishioner.

They just want to know if I'm donating to the cause.

Leaning over his laptop screen, he was about to dial the next church listed in the online Yellow Pages when he thought differently and slammed the phone back into its cradle.

"Wow," Carla said from behind, standing in the opposite side of the kitchen eating an apple and watching Doug fail miserably. "Having trouble finding Jesus?" Her sense of humor still retained her usual sarcasm, but where it was once coupled with light-hearted fun, it now doubled with doubt and despair.

He gave her a sharp look. "I'm glad this is funny for you."

She slurped a chunk of apple that nearly fell from her smiling lips.

"Sorry," she said robotically, and without remorse.

Doug sat down at the table in the center of the kitchen and rested his head against his hands. "Why will nobody help us?"

"Well," she began, "we've never been to church, Doug. What do you expect? You think they're just going to open their doors and say, 'Oh, yes, we'll bless your home. What else can we do for someone we've never seen before and will likely never see in our church again?'"

Doug sighed. "You're right." He nodded and stared out a window at the grey, sunless sky. "You're right."

"What if we just get some holy water and try blessing the house ourselves?"

"You mean, with prayers and stuff?" he asked.

She nodded. "Weren't you an altar boy or something when you were younger?"

Doug's eyes widened with doubt. "I don't remember any of those prayers, babe. I mean, I shook some bells when it was time, I grabbed the holy water and some stuff from a cabinet. I really don't remember much. Honestly, I hated church. Being an altar boy was my parents' way of giving me something to do during mass so I wasn't a bother to them."

"But you did assist with the holy water and stuff? Maybe the blessing of the Eucharist?"

Doug blinked slowly and incredulously. "Hon, that was like…twenty years ago."

"And you don't remember any of it?"

He shook his head.

"So we'll look some up. Can't be too hard."

"I don't know."

Carla stood quickly, her arms waving at her sides in frustration.

"Well, what else are we gonna do? Our seven-year-old daughter is freaking out almost nightly! Apparently there's some man who won't leave her room and he wants us out, too, or else…" Her face was scattered as she tried to think. "Shit, I don't know, Doug! Who knows what this thing wants, but it's tearing our family apart!"

Doug stood and ran to the other side of the table. He wrapped his arms around her and stroked her back. "It's all right," he said. "We'll figure this out."

As he held her, he heard a door open at the end of the hall.

Doug continued to hold Carla as he listened to the footsteps get closer and closer. He watched for Janie to enter the room. When she did, her face was blank and tired.

"Why is Mommy yelling?"

Carla turned away and wiped her eyes.

"It's okay," Doug said. "Mommy is just worried, that's all."

"Worried about what?" Janie asked.

Doug crouched low, at eye-level with Janie. "Were you playing in your room just now, J-Bird?"

"Yeah."

"Were you alone or were you playing with someone?"

Carla now faced Janie as well, anticipating her response.

"With someone," Janie said, her eyes coyly looking down.

"Was it Mr. Achak?"

"Yeah."

"How does Mr. Achak play with you?"

Janie shrugged.

"Does he touch you?" It disgusted Doug to even ask the question.

Janie's eyes shifted left and right, averting his question.

"Oh my god," Carla cried from behind Doug. "I can't listen to this. I have to...I have to take out something for dinner. There's meat downstairs. I--in the freezer." She was talking too fast, too excitedly.

Doug turned to her. "Babe, it's okay. I—"

"No," she refused, cutting him off as she reached the door to the basement. "It's not okay. Nothing is okay." She pulled open the door and stood at the top of the stairs. "You need to fix this, Doug, because I don't know how. I don't—"

It was as if a hard gust of wind crashed into her from behind. Doug watched as Carla's body folded slightly, her back arching in, head snapping backward, and arms flailing and reaching for safety. Her eyes were huge terror-filled orbs of white and blue. She screamed something that didn't sound like a word and more like a panicked yelp—a futile plea for a wall to appear or an arm to reach out and stop her from falling forward.

Doug was still getting to his feet as Carla's body had all but disappeared from view. He ran across the kitchen toward the open door to the basement. The sound of Carla's fingernails desperately scraping the walls as she fell spread white-hot adrenaline through his abdomen, his heart, out to his extremities and to his fingertips. He heard a series of crashes as her body made repeated and violent contact with the wall and stairs. And then he heard the sound of splintering, wood separating from wood, and screws tearing away from the construction. Doug reached the door and looked down.

Carla lay across the stairs on her back, her head against the far end of the staircase. She clutched onto the busted railing after having reached for it to break her fall, but it had ripped away and left gaping holes in the drywall. Doug silently prayed it had slowed her descent even just a little bit.

"Don't move!" he yelled as he ran down the stairs, carelessly missing steps along the way.

Carla's chest heaved up and down as she continued to hold the railing close to her. Doug dropped to his knees by her side and quickly assessed her. Nothing looked immediately broken—no bones had broken through the skin, no distensions.

He saw Janie staring down from the top of the stairs.

"Janie, can you take the ice cubes out of the freezer and put them into a little baggie?"

Janie nodded and quickly disappeared.

"Let go, let go," he urged Carla, pulling the railing from her hands. "I got you. Let go." She tentatively let go of the fractured railing and Doug threw her arms over his shoulders. "Where do you hurt?"

Carla grunted feebly. "Everywhere." Her voice was strained, almost a whisper.

"What feels broken?"

Carla took a few breaths, each one slightly deeper than the previous one. "I can't tell."

"Okay, I'm going to help you down to the basement floor," he said, and Carla eyed him nervously. "If you feel any pain—*any* pain—you tell me and I'll stop. Yes?"

Carla nodded.

Janie reappeared at the top of the stairs. She held a large Ziploc bag full of ice cubes. "Daddy..."

Doug looked up. "Thank you, Sweetie. Bring it down here, please? Your mother is hurt."

Janie walked down the carpeted stairs, carefully placing a sideways-turned foot on each step. "Mommy, are you okay?"

"I'm fine," Carla tried to say, but it came out as a painful grunt as Doug helped her from the stairs and onto the floor of their finished basement.

The lights were off, but the windows provided enough outside light for Doug to navigate off the staircase and onto the carpeted basement floor. Carla shifted her heels back and forth as Doug moved her into a flat position. He noticed a large red shiner developing on the right side of her forehead. He grabbed the bag of ice from Janie and pressed it against the injury.

"Shit!" Carla grimaced. "That f—" Even amid the pain and not knowing if anything was broken, she still had the wherewithal to curb herself from using the "F" word in front of Janie. "That friggin' stings!"

"What about your ribs?" Doug asked. "Did you hit them hard?"

"No," Carla gasped. "Mostly my hips and shoulders."

As she lay flat, Doug placed a hand on her right shoulder and squeezed her arm at intervals until he reached her fingers. "No pain?" he asked.

She shook her head.

"Okay, try bending your right knee."

Carla bent the leg slowly until her right foot was flat on the floor.

"Good?"

She nodded.

"Okay, try the left leg."

Janie watched from a kneeling position as Carla performed the same task with her left leg. She bent it until both feet were flat. Doug checked her left arm the same way he'd checked her right. "Bend your elbow," he said.

Carla appeared to do so with no difficulty.

"You hit anything else?" Doug asked. "Beside your head?"

"My ass," Carla said. This time she didn't care to filter her language in front of her daughter. She reached across her body and squeezed her right shoulder at different locations; front, side, back. "Seems fine. This one, too." She rolled both shoulders in small circles.

"Good," said Doug. "Wanna try sitting up?"

Without answering, Carla removed the bag of ice from her head, pressed her hands against the floor, and started to sit up. Her eyes squeezed tightly as the effort to sit up was countered by the pain in her head and lower back.

"Any pain when you breathe?" Doug asked.

Carla shook her head. "It's fine," she puffed through gritted teeth. She eventually made it into a sitting position and rested her arms over her knees. She checked the bag of ice for blood and pressed it against her head again.

"You're damn lucky," Doug said.

"Am I?" she asked.

Doug's lips curled into a sheepish half-smile

Good point.

"Mommy, you're okay!" Janie said happily. She crawled across the floor and hugged her mother tightly.

"I'm all right, Sweetie."

"Don't hug her too tightly," Doug said. "Mommy might have some bruises."

Janie let go. "I'm sorry, Mommy."

"It's okay, J-Bird. C'mere." She smiled as she wrapped her left arm around Janie and they held each other.

While Janie's head was down, Carla cut a sharp look at Doug. Her expression was grave as she shook her head slowly. Doug read her mind: This is not happening again.

"I know," he said. "I know."

This could have been Janie.

CHAPTER 22

Mass was over by the time Doug arrived at the church on Sunday and the chapel had completely emptied out. The wind roared past Doug's head and he pulled the edges of his hood closer to his ears. He walked the grounds a while, waiting for a member of the clergy to come outside. As he did, his thoughts ranged from that of absurdity (Who would consider him a rational man after hearing his story?) to complete fear and immediacy.

Or maybe he wouldn't need to explain anything. He needed advice, but more than anything else, he needed confirmation he was doing the right thing.

Across from the church, Doug saw a car parked in front of a smaller building—the rectory. Exhaust emitted lightly from the small sedan's muffler; someone had left the engine running, likely allowing the car to heat up while he or she was inside. Doug hurried to the building, wincing as the relentless wind opened another crack in his hand.

Suddenly, the door to the rectory opened and an older woman exited. She shivered as the cold air bit at her exposed skin and quickly turned to lock up. She was short, hunchback, and she wore a black cardigan sweater and dark green pants. Doug noticed she appeared to be in a hurry, probably to get into the waiting car.

When she turned and saw Doug standing there, she flinched.

"Whoa," she said, placing a hand over her chest. "You startled me."

"Sorry, uh...Ma'am?" Doug's afterthought of propriety was abrupt and forced.

"'Ma'am' is fine," she said with a kind smile. "Or you can call me Beatrice. I help out with the church, but I'm not a member of the clergy. If that's who you're looking for, of course."

Doug was relieved by her cordiality, but it didn't make what he wanted to ask any easier to do so.

"Mass is over," Beatrice prompted. "Can I help you with something?"

He approached her and extended his hand. "My name is Douglas Mitchell."

Beatrice took his hand in her own and squinted against the wind—a measure of preventing the cold blast from biting at her naked eyes.

"It's nice to meet you, Beatrice."

"Likewise," she said.

Her skin showed a soft, worn, and wrinkled appearance, and Doug guessed her to be about seventy years old. She had an endearing demeanor that made Doug feel as if he were talking to his late grandmother. He'd had a strong bond with his Nana, one he had continued to feel ever since she passed away eleven years prior; Beatrice's smile reminded Doug of the warmth with which his grandmother had once treated him.

Beatrice wore a gold cross around her neck, similar to the one he always saw around his Nana's neck, and Doug briefly wondered if it was something Beatrice wore all the time, or only to the church.

He let go of her hand and said, "I'm wondering if you can help me." Beatrice looked at him with attentive eyes. "Would I be able to take home some holy water with me?"

Beatrice's eyes widened as if she'd never received such an innocent request before, but not so much that it appeared she would simply dismiss it.

To Doug's surprise, she said, "Sure. Let's head back to the church."

The bitter February air ushered the two of them along quickly as Beatrice led Doug back to the church. He stuffed his hands into the pockets of his blue hooded parka and noticed Beatrice wore no coat of any kind, only the sweater. A small twinge of guilt poked his stomach as Doug realized he'd forgotten about the running car. She'd probably run into the rectory for some last-minute thing only to be intercepted by Doug.

He stopped.

"I'm sorry, is that your car? Do need you need to be somewhere?"

"It's fine," Beatrice said with a wave of her hand.

"You're sure?"

She nodded.

He continued to walk at her side, the guilt subsiding but only a little. The wind was low, but as she walked, Beatrice hunched forward—even further than the Kyphosis had already caused—with her arms folded across her body and her hands tucked into her sides.

"I appreciate the time, Beatrice," Doug said. The words sounded as if they'd been pushed from his mouth, forced out of obligation. He wondered if she had heard it, too.

"It's no problem at all," she said. "I had to head back to the church, anyway."

Doug stole a casual glance back at the rectory and noticed the considerable distance between it and the church, which felt even farther in the cold. If Beatrice *really* needed to go back to the church, Doug was sure she would have driven around the property and parked in the church lot.

As if reading his mind, Beatrice looked up at the sky's cold grey ceiling for the first time. Then she shrugged. "The cold doesn't really bother me."

They reached the church about a minute after leaving the rectory. It was rather nondescript and plain-looking by Doug's estimation. A small and red brick building, it resembled an old-fashioned schoolhouse—a rectangular frame under a sharp-angled roof. On top was a tall white steeple. The church's brick exterior was offset in the front by four square white pillars and a simple green hedgerow.

Beatrice reached for the handle of the church's double doors, but Doug grabbed it before her.

"Please, I insist."

"Thank you, Douglas," she smiled. He held the door open, allowed Beatrice to walk through, and then followed her inside.

The inside of the church was nearly as plain as the outside, but Doug felt a comfort that could only be described as "cozy." He followed Beatrice up the nave, between two rows of evenly spaced pews. He looked left and right, studying the artwork in the painted-glass windows. Doug recognized several of the images from his days as an altar boy: Jesus Christ standing with outstretched arms; the Virgin Mary cradling a newborn; a bleeding Jesus being helped down from the cross. Doug wondered if today's visit was going to help his situation at all.

When they reached the end of the nave, he stood and faced the altar. The sanctuary consisted of a single riser, the center of which featured the holy table. To the left of this was a small chancel—a single chair. Just to the side of the chair was a podium. There was no microphone, but given the tight interior, Doug presumed a speaker system was probably unnecessary.

Behind the altar was a larger-than-life-sized statue of Jesus in the same outstretched-arms pose Doug had seen in one of the windows. As if by reflex, he genuflected, made crosses over his forehead, lips and heart with his thumb, and stood up again. Beatrice then waved him politely up onto the sanctuary riser.

"This way," she said. She then turned and proceeded across the altar.

Doug followed her to the rear corner of the church and through a door that led into a small hallway. The hall was only about ten feet long with a ceiling low enough that if he jumped, Doug would have bumped his head. It was narrow too. Probably just wide enough to afford two people enough room to pass by each other, but only by turning sideways—and even by doing that, they'd still probably brush against each other.

At the end of the hall was a counter with a small sink and a bottle of generic, store-brand soap. To Doug's right were three wall-to-ceiling wooden lockers. One of the doors stood ajar and Doug caught a glimpse of a white robe. He quickly surmised that this was probably a mere closet at one time that was turned into a changing area for the priest.

Against the left-hand wall stood a very impressively-sculpted marble holy water font. There were leaves carved into and around the rim of the basin, which stood on a single, sturdy, and simply adorned pillar. In the Sistine Chapel, it would have been quite meager, but for the Heart of the Lake Church of Southwick, Massachusetts — aptly named for the body of water by which it stands — Doug was impressed.

"Isn't it beautiful?" Beatrice asked.

"It really is," Doug said with awe in his eyes. "I didn't expect something so..."

"Yes?"

"Elaborate. It's wonderful."

Beatrice nodded appreciatively. "It was a gift from our sister church in Springfield."

"Ah," Doug offered.

After a few moments of awkwardly admiring the structure, Beatrice broke the silence. "Do you have something to carry it out with, son?" she asked referring to the holy water.

"Oh, yes," Doug said. He fumbled through his pockets and produced a cup-sized plastic Tupperware container. He popped off the lid, leaned toward the font to collect some water and then hesitated. He straightened and turned toward Beatrice, holding the Tupperware in front of him. "Should I, or..."

"It's okay, dear, you can take some yourself."

Doug nodded shyly and turned back to the font, dunked the plastic receptacle into the water, allowing it to reach just below the Fill line and removed it. He placed the lid on top, meticulously sealing the container all along the edge until he was confident in the closure. When he was done, he looked up at Beatrice. She remained there, her hands clasped in front of her, smiling and patiently waiting for Doug to finish.

"I guess that's it," he said. His eyes darted around and the narrowness of the hallway stunned him once more. If he'd spread out both arms, he would have had to bend one elbow just to fit. He began to grow claustrophobic when Beatrice didn't respond right away, so he said, "Do I have to...I mean, can I take this now, or..."

The smile never left Beatrice's face. "If that's all you need son, then you may go with God."

Doug smiled back at her. His shoulders slackened as tension released from his muscles. He wasn't sure why he'd been so nervous to come to the church in the first place— probably out of fear he would be asked about the need for the holy water. But Beatrice never asked, neither with words nor gesture. And although she told him she wasn't part of the clergy, to Doug she appeared as much a servant of God as any priest or nun. He felt peaceful and safe in her presence, and in the church, and he began to wonder if attending service regularly would make him feel this way every week.

In his mind, he knew it was something he would talk to Carla about, after the activity either settled down or stopped completely. Doug never considered himself a spiritual person, but in that moment, he wondered why.

"Thank you, Beatrice," he said. "I really appreciate it. Shall we go back out the same way?"

Beatrice nodded.

Doug turned and walked back out into the church. He passed the holy table, stepped down from the altar and turned. He again genuflected in front of the cross and walked back through the nave toward the main entrance.

As he pushed the double doors, Doug felt a small object fall on his shoulder. He looked left, extending his arm so he could see his entire sleeve. Nothing. Then he looked down to the floor. A small, gold-colored circular medallion rested by his foot. He bent down to pick it up and realized it was a keychain. The medallion showed an embossed picture of an angel. Doug could also clearly make out some words along the edge of the small ornament:

"Don't be afraid, for there is a guardian angel watching you."

Doug stared at the words and read them again. Then again. Then a fourth time. His feet were rooted to the threshold as he stood in the open doorway between the church and the February air. Thoughts of spirits, and of those passed on and "watching over" him knotted his stomach and numbed his legs. Doug was never a believer in destiny or fate, but he was suspicious of strange and unlikely coincidences. And on a scale from one to ten of "strange and unlikely," Doug gave this a twelve.

He was still staring at the small trinket when Beatrice finally reached him. "What did you find, son?"

Her presence surprised him, but not so much that he flinched; he merely jerked his head slightly at the sound of her voice.

"I uh…" he stammered. "I just found this." He held out the medallion and she accepted it with one hand. Doug then looked up and studied the top of the door. "I think it fell or something. Does the priest or a member of the church keep that there for…" He almost said *good luck*. "For spiritual reasons?"

"I've never seen this before in my life," she said, staring at the small golden circle. Her tone was sturdy, confident—not cold, but not exactly warm, either. Doug wasn't sure if the medallion's appearance was a good or bad thing.

"I just sort of found it here," he rambled. "It fell and landed on my shoulder." He watched as the woman turned the medallion over in her hand, studied the back, then turned it on its front again and continued to study it. He swallowed hard. "Is that a good sign?"

Beatrice finally met his eyes and her smile returned. "Son," she said, "angels are good." She held out the medallion for Doug to take, but he resisted.

"Maybe you should keep it," he suggested. "Perhaps it belongs to a member of the church." He watched Beatrice's face work into an expression of pondering. "I'd be upset with myself if I took something that belonged to someone else. Who knows, maybe it's important to someone?"

"Could be," she said. "But then, if it *was* important, why would that person leave it at the top of a church door to potentially fall off and hit somebody?"

Doug opened his mouth to say something, then strained his brain to work out a reason. When he could think of none, he let out a sigh, his shoulders drooped.

"I don't know, I'm sorry." He stood awkwardly in the half-open door, waiting for Beatrice to say something. After a few moments, he decided to leave. "Well, I really must go. Thank you, Beatrice. For everything."

"You're welcome, Doug." Doug watched her place the medallion in the front pocket of her pants. "God be with you."

"And you as well."

CHAPTER 23

After failing to penetrate the cloud cover, the sun humbly crawled under the horizon and night fell over an otherwise uneventful afternoon. The February wind had slowed to a gentle whisper, calming the howling animal that had raged for most of the day. Carla's injuries had luckily amounted to nothing more than a few darkened bruises. The railing, though separated from the wall, had been enough to weaken her impact on the stairs. No broken bones, but her lower back showed a purple mark the size of a T-bone steak. The pain, however, was nothing six hundred milligrams of Ibuprofen couldn't fix. And then six hundred more several hours later.

Doug had produced the container of holy water upon arriving at home. When Janie asked what it was, Doug simply explained it was a "special" kind of water that would help (and he *hated* to recognize the entity's name in front of Janie) Mr. Achak find his way back to his real home. Janie's reaction had been sadness, but also of understanding. She told her parents she would miss her new friend, but she understood why it was time for him to go home.

After dinner, Doug, Carla, and Janie moved through the house together, stopping in each room and reciting some prayers Doug had remembered from his days serving as an altar boy. Doug's confidence in the ritual wasn't one hundred percent, but his philosophy had always been, "doing something is better than doing nothing," and it wouldn't hurt to try.

They spent the most time blessing Janie's bedroom; Doug purposely saved hers for last. In his mind, the entity seemed most comfortable in there, so it would make sense to "rid" all the other rooms of the ghost's presence first, thereby forcing it into Janie's room. From there, they would concentrate their prayers on that space. He'd only used about half the container of holy water on the rest of the house and planned to use the remaining quantity in her room.

Doug entered first. The same thickness he'd felt when he saw the apparition sitting on Janie's bed was there again. He seemed to be *pushing* into her room, forcing his way in, rather than walking into it. When he felt he'd established his own presence, he asked Carla and Janie to join him.

He placed a hand into the container of holy water.

"Our Father, who art in Heaven," he began. "Hallowed be thy name..." He reached out his moistened hand and splayed his fingers, flicking the water across the room. He spread the water on Janie's rocking chair, on the window—the sill, the glass, the curtains—and onto her bedspread. He threw some onto the shelf where the snow globe sat. He moved over to her closet and doused the edges of the door. Then he opened the door and splashed her clothes, her shoes, her belts, her backpack, and all of her dolls.

Doug approached all four corners of Janie's room, one at a time, and repeatedly doused each corner with the water.

I'll be damned if this thing hides out in any crevice of her room.

As an afterthought, he glanced upward toward the ceiling, dunked his hand into the remaining water, and flicked it above him. He did this many times until there were only a few drops of water left in the container. He turned the container upside down and randomly shook it outwardly. When it was empty, he rested it on Janie's bed, satisfied he'd covered her entire room.

He returned to the middle of the room, joined Carla and Janie again, and said, "Lord, please keep our family safe." He reached behind and found both Carla's and Janie's hands and clasped them in his own. "It is only our family who dwells here, nobody else."

He paused. Thoughts began to swirl in his head of what to do next, or what to say. How would he close their blessing? Would all they had attempted so far be enough?

Was he forgetting something? He felt he was missing something crucial, a critical part of the blessing that would ultimately remove the entity from the house for good.

As he pondered this, he felt his family's hands squeeze tightly around his own. He could tell by the force of their grips that they were terrified. They were waiting for something to happen; some kind of ending, an assurance that this was it, and they were now safe and alone in the house. But in this gesture, he also felt their unquestioning belief in him. They were depending on him. He knew they were counting on him to reclaim their home for all of them. It was through this recognition of his family's unconditional faith that he did the only thing he could think of.

He spoke directly to the spirit.

"If you're still here, you need to understand you are no longer welcome."

Carla's and Janie's grips tightened even more, crushing his hands and knuckles, forcing the blood from his fingers and up into his wrists. He wondered if their increased fear was in response to either the words he'd said or the coldness in his voice. He didn't waver and he spoke methodically. Suddenly, an unexpected feeling of peace and calm draped over him like a sheer cloth. He was no longer afraid.

"I cannot see you," Doug continued, "but I know you can see me." He squeezed Carla's and Janie's hands back just as tightly as they had his. "Now watch and listen to me as I say this: You are not wanted here. You were *never* wanted here." The conviction in his voice as he said the word "never" surprised even himself. "My daughter does not wish to play with you anymore. She is not your friend. She does not like you."

At this, Doug heard a small sniffle from behind and he turned to his right. He looked down and saw the tears in Janie's eyes, the slight hiccup in her chest as she sobbed. She didn't return his glance and he faced forward again.

"My daughter is hurt and scared by what you've done to our family. She never wants to see you again. She doesn't want to play with you again. None of us want to see you again. Please go. You are banished from this home."

Doug took a deep breath and turned to look at Carla. Her attention was on Janie, but she must have felt his gaze because her eyes slowly met his. Without a word, he nodded. Carla returned the gesture.

Before he let go of their hands, he issued one final statement: "We wish you peace as you leave this house." A sign of mercy. Of forgiveness.

Then he said, "Go with God."

He let go of his family's hands and made the sign of the cross.

They left the room.

CHAPTER 24

His eyelids fluttered. Doug caught the reddish, blurred-out numbers on the clock across the room and the hazy swell of the street light outside. He stared at the sheer curtains and took a breath; the moisture that escaped from his lips confounded him.

He suddenly noticed how cold his nose was, and how entangled in the comforter he'd become. Doug immediately found this strange. He'd loaded the stove with more coal than usual given the extreme low temperatures they'd been having all week. He hadn't seen the mercury get above twenty-six degrees during the day and the forecast on the news advised of temperatures falling into the single digits overnight.

It was too dark to read the temperature of the room on the electronic thermostat from the bed, but he guessed it was in the low fifties. Luckily the down comforter was still performing well; his body was warm from the neck down, but he felt the stubborn cold scrape at his ears and nose.

Don't tell me I've got a busted stove now.

Hours ago, he was confident he'd ridden their home of the spirit known as "Mr. Achak." The last thing he needed was for some kind of breakdown of any of their critical household appliances.

As he got out of the bed, his gaze went through the open door of their bedroom and straight at a waiting Janie standing in the hallway.

"J-Bird," he said, startled. "What's the matter, sweetheart? You cold?"

Janie nodded.

"I'm going to go look at the stove. You wanna jump in bed with Mommy where it's warm?"

She shook her head.

"Why not?"

"I can't."

Even with all they'd experienced, he still wasn't sure how to respond to that statement.

I can't.

After he replayed her response in his head, Doug caught the tiny hitch in her voice. It was then he also became aware of the wetness around her eyes and cheeks. She'd been crying.

"What do you mean, you can't? What's wrong, Hon?" He stepped away from the bed, but Janie took a step backward. Doug stopped. "Janie?"

"I can't come in the room."

Oh, shit...

Doug steeled himself before asking, "Why not?"

"Because Mr. Achak says I can't go in."

The words were giant fists that squeezed his lungs, his heart, and his soul. They were the words Doug had feared most. His head became light and Janie now appeared to be standing fifty feet away. He didn't even feel his lips move when he asked, "Why did Mr. Achak tell you that?"

"He said he doesn't like the water you brought into the house." She was sobbing harder now. "He said you shouldn't have done that—that it was wrong of you to do."

"What's wrong?" Carla asked. She was now awake and kneeling in the bed behind Doug.

"Mr. Achak doesn't like Daddy's water!"

Janie was becoming hysterical and Doug could hear the pleading in her voice. She wanted Doug to reverse what he'd done.

What kind of spiritual entity doesn't like holy water? Doug thought to himself. He tried to rationalize an explanation in his head but came up empty. Then...

Oh my god.

"Doug? Wha—?" Carla began, but Doug waved her off.

"Janie?" Doug said. "If I leave the room, will Mr. Achak let you come in and stay with Mommy?"

Janie looked down the hall, back toward her bedroom. As Doug watched her, he began to hear footsteps down the hall. They were slow and ominous. Calculating. Each step stoked the fire of anxiety that burned inside him. Though it was cold in the room, Doug felt beads of sweat form at his hairline. He felt Carla's hand reach for his and he tried to put every ounce of comfort into his grip as he squeezed back.

The footsteps came closer. Closer. Finally, they stopped. Janie's eyes now looked upward at an angle. Assuming she was meeting the entity's eyes, Doug estimated the ghost to be about as tall as him, if not a few inches taller.

In that moment, fear and pride collided as Doug watched his only daughter stand alone but firm in the presence of the spirit. With tears on her face, she never trembled and her eyes remained steady. And when she nodded, confirming receipt of some message, she did so slowly and deliberately.

She then faced her father again.

"He said yes."

Doug only became aware he'd been holding his breath after a long exhale, the moisture from his lungs momentarily clouding his view of his daughter.

"Okay," he said. "I'm going out into the hallway. After that, you come in here and I'll go talk to Mr. Achak."

Janie again looked upward at the being invisible to Doug and Carla. Then she turned to Doug once more and nodded.

Doug had to pull his hand away from Carla's as he got out of bed and moved slowly into the hallway. He stepped to Janie's left and unconsciously leaned out of the way so as not to bump into whatever was standing in the hallway next to his daughter. When he was completely free of the room, Janie walked in. Carla reached from the bed and pulled her in close. Doug looked in on the two of them.

Not knowing what else to say, he simply offered, "I'll be back when I can."

Doug set his eyes on the doorway to Janie's bedroom. It might as well have been the gates of hell. His heart, which had been thumping since he first saw Janie standing in the hall, now beat rapidly; a constant burning was all he could feel in his chest as he moved down the hall toward his daughter's room.

As he walked, Doug felt a presence over his right shoulder. It then moved to his left shoulder. Then back to the right. It was as if the spirit was taunting him, challenging him to enter Janie's room, and daring him to try and stop it.

At one point, Doug thought he felt a hot breath snarling down his neck, but it easily could have been his nerves firing hotter than at any time in his life. He was trying to save his family from this torture. Their way of life was now being threatened by some unseen force that was much stronger than any prayer Doug could have spoken.

He reached Janie's room. Inside it looked just as normal as it ever did. Amazing, Doug thought, how everything about their lives appeared normal on the surface. Yet underneath, there lurked something dark and sinister. And although unprepared, he was about to face the unknown with no ammunition except for the love of his family and his fear for their safety.

He walked inside and stood at the center of Janie's room, just as he did during the blessing. His throat was dry and he swallowed hard, trying to produce some saliva.

"Why are you here?"

His voice was brittle, his words frail, and they fell like silent ashes over Janie's room. He scolded himself for showing weakness, forced his hands into fists, and tried again.

"Who are you? Why are you here?"

More conviction this time—more bark and far more strength—but Doug still wasn't convinced he was fooling anyone. Certainly not himself. But it didn't matter now. His first two attempts to convey any kind of courage had failed. He could only stand there and wait for a response.

A cold air brushed against his hip and moved from back to front. Doug couldn't fight the shudder that quaked through his body.

Is that you?

By way of response, a voice no more than two inches from his face whispered:

"*Ahhh.*"

Doug struggled to maintain his breathing with steadiness and control. "Do you want to tell me something?"

Instead of a breath, this time, the response was much clearer:

"*Leave.*"

Again the word was spoken directly in front of him, and he felt he was staring into the entity's eyes. Tsunamis of blood swelled through his veins as his pulse threatened to overtake any resolve he had left.

Doug stood firm and managed a half-hearted, "No." And like before, he regrouped quickly and tried to speak in a stronger tone. "This is my home. My family's home. You don't belong here. You're not wanted here." Doug waited several seconds for a response. Before he received one, he said, "It's time for *you* to leave."

The emphasis on *you* had been unintentional and Doug feared retaliation. He noticed a slight change in the air around him, as if the pressure had shifted. As if the thing that once stood before him had moved. Doug wondered if it was leaving. Then he heard the unmistakable sound of a mattress sinking underweight. In the dark, Doug saw a large depression form on Janie's bed, much like the day he first saw the entity. The woman. And it suddenly occurred to Doug the entity in the room now felt much more masculine and more aggressive.

"That's not yours," Doug warned. "Get off. That is where my daughter sleeps."

"*Mine*," the voice responded.

"No," Doug demanded. "That belongs to my daughter. It's not yours. None of this is yours," he said with a wave of his hand. "It's time for you to go."

"*Mine*," the voice repeated.

"No! This place is not yours! This is our home and you're not allowed here!"

"*MINE!*"

A blast of cold air rushed against Doug's chest and arms. It lifted him off his feet and sent him across Janie's room. His body slammed against the closet doors and he fell to the floor in a heap of confused terror.

"Daddy!" Janie cried from down the hall.

From a prone position, Doug shouted toward the open door: "Stay with Mommy!"

He returned his attention to the bed. The depression in the mattress was gone. The presence of whatever had knocked him across the room took shape in the form of a mass in front of him — black, faceless, but nonetheless human. Doug raised himself up on his elbows but didn't dare stand up to the thing, not yet.

He studied the mass in front of him. It wasn't the great, hulking figure Doug had expected. The figure was very close to his size; average in height and build. By all accounts, he probably shouldn't have feared the entity, but the thing possessed a strength he had never known before, and he wasn't ready to challenge it.

Doug tried to think quickly. His family wouldn't be spending the rest of the night in their home. He would have to collect them and leave, assuming the ghost was going to let him leave Janie's room.

Doug stared into the mass. It hadn't moved an inch since it presented itself. Slowly, he pulled his feet underneath him one at a time. Then he pushed off the floor with his hands and eventually returned to a standing position.

"Fine," he said, his voice dripping with defiance. "We will leave tonight."

He waited for a response but there was none. He turned to the door and headed toward the hallway. He expected to feel a pair of hands grip his shirt from behind and pull him back into the room, but the entity let him go without contest.

When Doug reached the hall, he turned and ran toward his bedroom. Carla and Janie sat huddled together on the bed.

"We're leaving," he said. "Now."

"Doug," Carla said, "where are we going to—"

"Now!" he shouted, cutting her off. He grabbed a sweater from his dresser and pulled a couple pairs of jeans from the closet. He tossed one to the bed. "Here, get dressed," he said as he yanked his jeans over his pajama pants.

Carla climbed from the bed and began dressing. Doug hastily worked the sweater over his head and stuck his arms through the sleeves. Then he noticed Janie sitting alone on the bed. She was hysterical.

"Oh, J-Bird," he said rushing to her. He climbed onto the bed and pulled her to him. "I'm sorry, baby. I'm sorry. But we have to go. It's best if we leave tonight."

"Where will we go?" she asked between sobs.

Doug stopped for a second. He hadn't time to think about it until just now. Then, the most logical choice entered his mind.

"We'll go to Uncle Luke and Aunt Diane's. You can sleep with your cousins." He caressed her face, moved her brown locks behind her ears. "Does that sound good?" Janie nodded, her body shuddering from crying so hard. "Okay, good." He looked to Carla. She was stretching a pair of heavy socks over her bare feet. "Are you ready?"

"Yeah," she said. "I just have to go to Janie's room and get—"

"No, uh uh," he said. "Nobody's going into her room."

"But Doug, it's freezing! What's she going to wear?"

"Her winter coat is in the hallway closet. She can wear that."

"Doug…"

"She's only going to be outside for a few minutes. After that, the heat in the car will keep us warm. Five minutes in cold air isn't going to kill anyone. Besides, Luke's is right down the street. We'll be there before she has a chance to even feel cold."

Carla put up her hands in surrender. "Fine. Let's go."

"Okay." Doug looked at his daughter. "Ready, Sweetie? We're going to go to your Aunt and Uncle's now."

Janie nodded.

Doug picked her up and moved off the bed. He and Janie were first to leave the bedroom. Carla stayed close behind. Doug didn't bother to look into Janie's room as he hurried by, but he felt her head twist and crane against his shoulders as he passed.

"Don't look, Sweetie. It won't hurt you as long as I've got you." He didn't believe it to be true, but he felt in his heart she should hear him say it.

He reached the closet at the end of the hall just before the kitchen. He ripped open the door and grabbed Carla's and Janie's matching periwinkle parkas. He handed Carla hers and worked Janie's coat around her and zipped it up the front.

"This is just for a little bit," he told Janie. "Before you know it, we'll be with your cousins where it's safe. And warm!" He forced a smile, which Janie saw, though it didn't do much to stop her tears.

Doug handed Janie to Carla while he found his coat. He quickly shoved his hands into the sleeves, pulled the coat on over his shoulders, and zipped up. He then took Janie back into his arms.

"Okay, let's go."

They moved through the kitchen as one. Janie held on to Doug, her arms wrapped tightly around his shoulders, while Carla kept pace behind them leaving little space between her and her husband. Doug rushed past the breakfast bar and down into the foyer, swiping a set of keys off the bar before opening the front door. He let Carla through first, then moved outside. Holding Janie close with one arm, he reached back with the other to close the door.

As he did, an image in the great room caught his eye. A black mass stood in front of the coal stove—the same black mass that had chased him from Janie's room. Rage boiled inside him and Doug paused. He considered going back inside and unleashing a verbal fury on the thing. The anger and fear he felt then compared to no emotion he'd ever experienced in his life. But shouting would serve no use. Screaming out loud was not going to make it go away.

Defeated, and with great reluctance, Doug feebly clenched his teeth, gripped the door handle with white knuckles, and pulled it shut.

CHAPTER 25

Doug stared into his swirling cup of Columbian coffee. It was four-thirty in the morning and he hadn't slept a minute since they'd arrived at Luke and Diane's house. Janie wanted to sleep in the kids' room, but Doug and Carla had said it was too late and they didn't want to risk waking her cousins, so she slept with Carla in the guest room. Doug attempted to sleep on the couch, but replays of Janie standing in his bedroom doorway, and of his interaction with the entity, played on a loop in his memory. Even with his eyes shut, it was as if they were still open; the images retained in them having never left the forefront of his mind.

It wasn't long after he'd moved into his brother's kitchen, turned on the Keurig, and popped in a K-Cup, that his sister-in-law appeared next to him. He apologized profusely for waking her and insisted she go back to bed, but Diane asserted it was not because of Doug's actions that she was awake. She claimed she also couldn't sleep.

"I just felt like I needed a coffee," she explained.

Doug knew it was an innocent deception, but he wasn't about to call her out for lying. Especially since he desperately wanted the company of someone not directly tied to his family's experiences.

He was twirling a spoon in his cup, forcing the hot liquid into a tiny, light-brown whirlpool when Diane broke the silence again.

"You're never going to sleep if you keep stirring that."

Doug looked up with red-streaked eyes. His face conveyed all he needed to say without speaking a word.

"I know, I know," Diane conceded. "Just trying to lighten the mood."

"You're right," Doug sighed. "It's just frustrating—no, demoralizing—not to be able to stop what's happening to my family. I'm supposed to be the head of my family, Diane! The protector! I should be winning this fight, but instead...I'm losing, and it's because I have no idea *how* to fight back." Tears formed at the rims of his eyes.

"You still haven't told me or Luke what exactly happened tonight."

Doug looked away and nodded pensively. "You wouldn't believe me if I tried to explain."

"Try me."

After a moment's hesitation, Doug recapped the last few months of activity in greater detail than the last time he had seen Diane, concluding with a very vivid account of the events that took place in his home hours before their arrival at her and Luke's house.

Diane stared at him, slack-jawed.

"I told you," Doug reminded her.

"Holy shit, Doug. This all really happened? And did Carla see a doctor when she fell—when she was pushed down the stairs?"

Doug laughed weakly. "She probably should have but...I don't know...it's just been hectic lately, you know? Just too much going on, too much on our minds."

He watched Diane's face turn from concern to ire and he held up a defensive hand.

"Don't worry," he insisted. "I checked her thoroughly. She didn't break anything—just got some nice bruises."

"Doug, I'm serious."

Doug shot Diane a level stare. "She's fine. Trust me. If there's one thing that woman knows, it's when not to mess around with your health."

"Mm," Diane agreed.

The two of them sat quietly. Doug took a prolonged sip from his coffee. His eyes darted around the kitchen and in his nonstop periphery he could see Diane staring at him intently. Her fingers tapped alongside her cup, demanding of something Doug left unsaid, and of which he'd hoped not to speak, but his sister-in-law's gaze was like that of a bull threatening to charge. Finally, he gave in.

"What is it?"

She studied him a bit longer after his eyes met hers. "There's something else, isn't there?"

"No, that's pretty much all of it."

"No," she insisted. "If that was it, you would have rushed your wife to the hospital after she fell down a flight of stairs. There's more. Tell me."

Doug sighed and rolled his eyes when he realized he'd been made.

"God, you're like a friggin' shrink or something."

"Thanks. I minored in psychology. Now what is it?"

Doug's shoulders, once tensed and raised to his neck, finally dropped and rested. He inhaled and exhaled deeply, much like someone does just before they're about to divulge a hidden piece of information. He stared right at her, and when he did, his eyes shook with fear. He noticed even she shifted uncomfortably with nervous anticipation of what he was about to tell her.

It had been on his mind ever since Janie said it—when he had left her with Carla and walked into her room. When he had faced the spirit. It was what had kept him awake all these hours, and what he expected would keep him awake for many months to come. It was the thing he didn't want to speak about out loud because, in his thoughts, it was already too scary. Saying it out loud would only make it scarier...because it would become that much more real. It might have been the one thing to sever the last frayed and withered threads of his sanity.

"Diane..." His voice, barely above a whisper, wavered like paper shreds floating in front of an oscillating fan.

"Yes?"

"What kind of spirit does not like holy water?"

"Doug..."

"What?" he asked again, but not expecting her to guess.

"Doug, stop..."

"What is it, Diane?" The panic in his voice, as well as the volume, began to climb. "Huh? What kind of *thing*," he continued, driving his finger into the tabletop, "does *not* like holy water???"

Diane grabbed his hand. "Shh, you're going to wake everybody up."

He was crying hard now. "Why, Diane? Why did it choose us?"

"I don't know, Doug." She held his hand and massaged the top of it with her own. "It's not fair and your family deserves better."

He pressed his other hand against his face, squeezing the tears from his eyes.

"What matters right now," she continued, "is that the three of you are safe, and you can stay here as long as you need to. Luke and I already talked about it, shortly after you guys got here."

Doug pulled his free hand away from his face and looked at her. His voice was barely audible. "Thank you."

"You're family," Diane said. "This is what families do."

She continued to massage his hand while Doug's sobs slowed and his breathing started to come back to normal. He took another sip of coffee and winced—it had cooled off considerably.

"Dump that out," Diane said. "Go get another one."

He waved her off. "Nah, I'm good. I really don't need another one."

"You sure?"

Doug nodded.

Diane watched him in silence as his eyes betrayed his thoughts. Rather than ask another question right away, she got up from the table, walked over to a cabinet and pulled out a package of sugar cookies. She brought it back to the table and opened it. Their kitchen was enormous; an island stood in the middle and great, cavernous twelve-foot ceilings rose above. The crinkle of the foil cookie package echoed off the high ceilings, walls, and cabinetry. Diane pulled out a cookie and bit from it. She offered the package to Doug and he reached in for one.

"So," she said without further strategic delay, "are you guys going to move out?"

Doug put the whole cookie in his mouth and shrugged. "Can't really do that," he said between chewing.

"Why not?"

"Since the market tanked, we're barely above water. We'd be lucky just to break even right now if we sold the house. And even if we did, we wouldn't have anything to use as a down payment on a new place."

"You guys have been there a long time though. You must have some equity by now?"

"Hmph, you would think so. Except we financed one hundred percent."

"Shit."

"Yeah, I know. So as we've been paying down the mortgage, so has the home's value gone down."

"Aren't there programs though?"

"Yes. In fact, we refinanced just before all this shit started happening. Then we found out that banks won't even talk to you until at least a year after you've refi'd."

"Ouch."

"Eh, it wasn't an issue at the time. Now…" He paused and shook his head. "I just don't know what to do."

"What if you took the hit and rented for a while?"

"I don't want to rent. Janie needs a yard. She loves our backyard and she loves her room. I can't take that away from her."

"Even if it was temporary?"

Doug shook his head. "She deserves that house. And I'm not going to let that…whatever it is…take it away from her either. It's hers."

Diane smiled. "Well I'm glad to hear some resolve in your voice again." For the first time that night, Doug smiled back at her. "I was starting to think we were losing you, Douglas Mitchell."

He laughed. "I know when I'm beaten," he said. "I just haven't figured out how to win yet."

She winked at him. "That's our boy."

Doug laughed even harder this time.

"Sorry," she said. "Luke's whole 'big brother' mentality rubs off on me at times."

Doug stood from the table, walked around to where Diane sat, and hugged her. "Thanks, Diane."

She hugged him back. "Aw, shucks. 'Twas nothing."

He backed off and looked her in the eye. "I mean it."

She smiled back at him. "I know. And you don't have to thank me."

Doug finally let go and said, "Maybe not, but I do have to try to get *some* sleep. And so do you. Go on, get to bed."

"All right, fine. You talked me into it."

Doug emptied his coffee in the sink and placed the cup in the dishwasher.

As he was about to leave the kitchen, Diane said, "By the way, I may have another option for solving your problem."

Doug stopped, turned around. "Oh, yeah? What's that?"

"Well," she began. "Since the holy water didn't seem to help, I may know someone who can."

"Really? Who?"

"Just some people who know about these things."

"Really? How do they help?"

"Let's just say they're into alternative methods."

CHAPTER 26

Even with barely two hours sleep, Doug managed to see Janie off on the school bus outside Luke and Diane's house. He had even driven Carla back home in time to welcome the daycare parents and their children. He and Carla felt that without Janie in the house, the spirit would be less active and the home would be safer for the kids. Besides, the last thing Carla wanted to do was close the daycare and risk the indignation of her parents.

He sat in his cube at work and stared at the pictures of his family adorning his desk. There was an old one of Janie wearing a helmet far too large for her tiny head and pedaling a tricycle for the first time. Next to that was a more recent one taken during a camping trip the previous summer: Carla and Janie were in a tent, on top of a pile of sleeping bags, and laughing after a spirited tickle-torture.

As he slumped forward against his desk, Doug reached into his pocket and pulled out a slip of paper. A phone number was written on it. His thoughts immediately went to Diane's words from earlier that morning.

"Their names are Teresa and Alix," Diane had said. "They're mediums. Teresa is older. She has more experience. Alix helps, too; she's good, and goes with Teresa to every session. But Teresa is very, uh…let's say 'in tune,' and she does most of the heavy lifting."

"What's a medium?" Doug had asked. "How's she supposed to help us?"

"A medium serves as a conduit between our world and the spirit world. She's good, trust me."

"So, what…she talks to dead people, or something?"

"You're just like your older brother," she sighed. "And it's not that simple. I'm just saying: The holy water thing obviously didn't work. No priest seems to want to help you out, so what can it hurt? Give 'em a call. They'd probably be able to come to your house same day, maybe next day."

Doug let out a dubious murmur.

"Just call them, Doug. It'll be good for you guys."

"Fine, fine. I'll call 'Madame' Teresa and her handler, Alix."

"You know," Diane said, "given the circumstances, it's good to hear any humor out of you at all."

Doug stayed quiet and simply eyed her suspiciously.

"Otherwise," she continued, "I'd kick your ass."

He smirked. He'd always enjoyed Diane's wit and her overall sense of propriety. When he was in seventh grade and she and Luke were seniors in high school, Doug had secretly had a crush on Diane. He never told her or Luke, but he suspected Diane knew. As he got older and more mature, he still retained a shadow of that former crush—more of an admiration, really—but he never acted on it. He was never jealous of Luke. In fact, he was never anything but happy for his older brother. He simply knew when he found the woman of his dreams, he wanted her to be just like Diane. When Carla entered his life, he knew she was the one and he held on, never to let go.

Doug hesitated before asking the next question; he wasn't sure he wanted to know the answer.

"What makes you so confident they can help? How do you know these people?"

"I met them both a long time ago," Diane said. "Alix was in her early twenties. Teresa was already into her fifties. They're nice people. They helped me out a lot."

"Oh yeah? How so?"

Diane laughed. "That is a story for another time. Right now, you're going to be late, and Carla's kids will be sad if she's not there. Go!"

Doug opted to place the call outside, out of earshot of his co-workers.

After he left the main entrance to his office, Doug turned left and headed toward a group of picnic tables set out on the front lawn of the building. It was only ten-thirty a.m., far too early for lunch. It was unlikely any unwanted visitors would stop by while he was on the phone.

He removed his cell phone from his pocket, slid the unlock bar, and tapped the number into the keypad. It rang three times before a woman picked up.

"Hello?" said a voice that sounded much younger than Doug had expected. High and sweet. Diane had said the women were in their 20s and 50s when she met them, but that was a long time ago. By Doug's estimation, the voice on the other end of the line could have passed for twenty today.

"Um, hi," Doug stammered. "Er...is this Teresa?"

"Sorry, Teresa is busy at the moment. Can I take a message?"

This must be Alix.

"Is this Alix?" he asked.

"Yes," she said. Her voice now sounded a bit cautious. "Who's calling, please?"

"Sorry, my name is Doug Mitchell. I got your number from my sister-in-law, Diane Mitchell."

"Hmm, Diane..." Alix began as she searched her memory banks. "I'm afraid I don't know a Diane Mitchell."

Doug's heart sank.

"Wait! Diane Parsons?"

"Yes," Doug said. "I believe Parsons is her maiden name."

"Oh, yes, I know Diane. *We* know Diane. Haven't spoken to her in over a year now. How is she?"

"She's great. Actually, my family and I saw her last night."

"Oh, that's wonderful. Do tell her I said hello?"

Doug noticed her voice had once again turned warm and friendly, as if he were talking to the mother of a close friend.

"I absolutely will."

He waited a moment for Alix to say something else, only to realize she was waiting for him to do the exact same thing.

"Uh, I don't really know how to say this, but Diane gave me your number because some…things…have been happening in my home. These things are affecting my family, especially my seven-year-old daughter."

"Oh dear."

"I'm hoping that either you or Teresa—or both—can help me."

"What kinds of things, Doug?"

He went on to describe the last several months exactly as he did the night before for Diane. Throughout his description, he caught Alix saying things like, "mm hmm," and "okay, yes," as though she were keeping detailed notes on the entire conversation. She was easy to talk to and seemed genuinely concerned with what was going on. For the first time since the activity started, Doug felt he was sharing symptoms with a doctor, someone who could diagnose the problem and help fix it. He was surprised when he actually felt his lips curl into a smile as he spoke.

"Tell me about your home, Doug—where it is, if it's a new construction, what town…"

Doug told Alix about their home and the new foundation on which it was built—that the land was previously owned. He also told her what he found out from Esther, about Vera and her second husband, and how they both perished in the fire that destroyed their home.

"Oh, my. How sad. And what kind of people were they?"

Doug then went into Vera's story, as much as he could remember from what Esther had told him, and about her previous life as a missionary. He also told her about Vera's first husband, Edgar, and how he was killed in Sumatra.

"She even wrote a book about him," Doug said. He gave Alix the title.

"Interesting." There was another slight pause and Doug could hear a pencil working against a piece of paper. "I'm not familiar with it," Alix continued. "Have you read the book? Do you know what it talks about?"

"No. Why, do you think it's relevant?"

"I'm not sure. I'll see if I can locate a copy, you never know. Whenever there's this deep of a history involved, it helps to obtain as much information as possible. It's like they say about car insurance: 'it's better to have too much than not enough.'"

"Makes sense," Doug said.

"Can you spell Vera's last name for me?"

"O-L-U-M."

Alix spoke the name a few times, allowing the letters and consonants to roll over her lips. Then she asked, "Are you and your family around tomorrow night?"

"Tomorrow? Oh, um…"

"Is that too soon?"

"Oh, no, not at all; the sooner the better. I just didn't expect you'd be available so quickly."

"Well, when there's a child involved, Teresa and I like to get out to the location as soon as possible."

"I appreciate that."

"Mm-hmm. What's your address, Doug?"

Doug gave it to her and listened to Alix repeat the address as she wrote it down.

"Listen," he said. "I can't tell you how much I appreciate your and Teresa's help."

"You're very welcome, Doug. The fact that you're calling means one of two things: that you're either a believer in our kind of healing, or that you're desperate and have nowhere left to turn. So let me just tell you this: Teresa is the real deal. I have abilities similar to hers, but Teresa has a true gift."

"Okay," he said, hanging on every word.

"She's aware that very few people have been given this gift. She's also aware that very few have such a *refined* gift as she. And so it's her pleasure to help others in need. It's her way of paying back, or forward, the gift of having such an amazing ability."

"Well that's awfully nice of her."

"It truly is."

Doug heard the reverence in her voice and couldn't help the warm feeling that brightened his heart.

"So, I guess we'll see you tomorrow night?"

"See you tomorrow night," Alix said. "About six-thirty p.m.? Does that work?"

"That works fine."

"Perfect. And Doug…"

"Yes?"

"Do something fun with your family tonight. Go out to dinner. See a movie. Anything that will take your mind off of things. And most importantly, try to get some rest. Tomorrow is going to be a long night."

CHAPTER 27

Six twenty-eight p.m.

Sitting on the sofa in their great room, Doug's left heel bounced on the floor, pivoting on the ball of his foot and causing his knee to rise and fall rapidly with the motion of a paddle ball. He hadn't realized he was doing it until Carla placed a calming hand on his leg.

"It's okay," she said.

His foot stopped jumping. He caught his breath and practiced a few deep ones. Inhale...exhale...inhale...exhale. He turned to Carla. He searched her eyes for any ambivalence toward what was about to happen. *God bless her*, he thought. She was trying like hell to put up a front. And she almost succeeded, but he saw it. Behind her eyes he saw a frightened little girl hiding under her bed sheets, hoping for the monster to go away.

He said nothing in response. He only concentrated hard on relaxing every muscle in his face, neck, and shoulders. When it didn't work, he thought of his little girl, playing with her cousins—she would stay with Luke and Diane tonight—having no idea what was happening inside her home. He smiled. Carla smiled back and squeezed his hand with both of hers. Doug nodded slowly. In that simple gesture, and without speaking a word, he'd said, "We're going to be fine."

He wasn't sure if he believed it, but it was as much as he could manage just to try to fool her.

Six-thirty p.m.

The soft, punctual knock at the door let loose a flood of questions in Doug's mind.

Is this really going to work? Are these people legit? Are they going to ask me for money? What if it doesn't work? What if they are *legit and they think we're all fools, that we've wasted their time?*

There was a brief moment's relief as Doug thought about Janie. Even during this time of doubt and fear, he was able to find a bit of comfort in knowing his daughter wouldn't have to see him like this; the worry and uncertainty on his face, the shaking of his hands, biting of his fingernails and irregular breathing. For months he'd been her rock. This was the first time he'd allowed the terror and emotion he'd kept locked inside to overcome him. For Doug, it was tantamount to failing at grieving over the passing of a loved one. So many times he'd wanted to give in to the pressure and just let it quake and tremble through his bones. But he couldn't. Not for Carla. Especially not for Janie.

Doug stood from the sofa, moved to the door and turned the handle. Two women stood outside on the front steps. The one on the left appeared markedly older than the other, but judging by her stance she seemed a sturdy old woman with plenty of good life left in her. Doug immediately picked her out as Teresa. She wore a wine-colored scarf that wrapped twice around her neck and fell down over a long black coat. Her hair was light, not quite blonde anymore, but not yet fully white, either. Her bluish-green eyes were friendly and honest; he immediately felt much more relaxed than he had only thirty seconds ago.

"You must be Teresa," he said, reaching out a hand.

She accepted his hand and shook it firmly. "Very nice to meet you, Mr. Mitchell."

He laughed nervously. "Please, Doug is just fine." He let go of her hand and turned to the woman at her side. "Alix? We spoke on the phone," he said, extending his hand once again.

She wore brown glasses that complimented her features. Her hair was dark like Carla's, but straight, and fell just below her jaw line. She had a youthful appearance—soft skin, hardly any visible lines around her eyes. From what Diane told him, Doug had assumed Alix to be in her forties by now, maybe even early fifties. However, if she was in fact in her fifties, Doug figured she could easily pass for forty if not younger.

"Yes, we did," Alix said with a big smile. As she shook his hand, Doug noticed a black leather satchel slung over her shoulder. "Pleasure to meet you in person."

"Likewise. Please, come in," Doug said, standing to the side and holding the door for them. The two women walked in, and just as soon as they began to remove their coats, their eyes looked off, as if searching for something. Doug caught it and immediately looked over to Carla. She'd caught it too.

"You have a lovely home," Teresa said breaking the silence.

Carla stood from the sofa. "Thank you so much," she said, shaking their hands. "I'm Carla. Thank you for coming. May I take your coats?"

Teresa and Alix both thanked her and handed over their coats.

Carla motioned to the sofa. "Please, make yourselves at home." She then disappeared down the hallway and the two women sat down.

Doug pulled the hassock away from the recliner and sat across from them. The three of them exchanged formal pleasantries—*Was it a long drive? Did you have much traffic? This is a lovely town.*—until Carla returned.

"May I get you both something to drink?" she asked. "I just boiled some water for tea."

"Tea sounds wonderful, dear," Teresa said. "And if you have any sugar, I'll take a teaspoon, if it's not too much trouble."

"Not at all. Alix?"

"A glass of water, please."

As she turned toward the kitchen, Carla talked over her shoulder. "So did Doug tell you what's been going on?"

"He did," Alix said. "I kept copious notes of our entire conversation."

"Did you share everything with Teresa?" Doug asked.

"A bit," Teresa nodded. "Although I have to be honest, we get calls like this quite often. Sometimes from dishonest folks only looking to have a little fun at our expense."

Carla walked into the room with their drinks.

"Thanks, dear," Teresa said, taking a small mug from Carla's hand. She then turned back to Doug. "So, please don't be offended that I chose not to speak with you over the phone."

"I wasn't offended at all. I can understand your hesitance."

Carla walked across the room and dragged the recliner next to her husband. "Doug told me what he told you and I couldn't help but think you two would consider us a couple of crazy people."

Alix turned to her and smiled. "Of course not. We take every case seriously. We hear what is said and we try to evaluate the person's motives, if any, by asking a lot of questions, just like I did on the phone with Doug. Questions like the history of the house and the land, how many members in the family, members who are being affected, specifically, and so on." Carla nodded intently as Alix continued. "We can usually figure out the false claims right off the bat."

"Wow," Doug said. "That's intuitive. But I guess you couldn't do what you do without a keen sense of intuition, huh?"

"It's a little more complicated than intuition," Teresa interjected, although she didn't say it to be defensive, but to merely add a point of clarification. "As a medium, I'm able to hear, see, and feel things beyond our world." She waved a hand toward Alix. "Both of us can."

Doug leaned forward. "How does it work? If you don't mind my asking."

Teresa placed her hands in her lap. "Not at all. We all have a sixth sense. It's a kind of extrasensory perception—ESP. For some, this sense is stronger than it is in others. With my ability, I've been able to assist police departments across the entire country with finding missing people."

"That's pretty amazing," Doug said. "Any success stories?"

"Quite a few, in fact," she said with much pride and no arrogance. "By the way, I should probably tell you that your daughter's connection to the spirit world is quite strong."

Doug stiffened at the thought. He wasn't comfortable with Janie having any sort of connection to the spirit world.

"It's okay," Teresa continued. "It's perfectly natural. It's a gift, actually. And she may carry this gift into her adulthood, or she may lose it, either by choice or by chance. Regardless of which, it's *because* of this gift that she's being visited by these spirits."

"Even if she doesn't want them here?" Doug asked.

"Consciously, she may not want them here, but subconsciously her mind is open, far more than most. The spirits are aware of this openness and they come to her."

Even when he referred to *them*, Doug wasn't aware he'd pluralized the entity in their home. It wasn't until Teresa had said *they* that an icy thought formed in his head. The medium was talking about more than one spirit.

He paused before asking his next question. The words had formed in his mind, but he needed a deep breath before bringing them to his lips.

"Teresa? I notice we're talking about this with the assumption that there's more than one spirit here."

Teresa nodded as if she and Doug had been on the same page since she and Alix had arrived.

"Right..." Doug said, cutting a nervous look toward Carla. "So, are you saying there's more than..." His voice stumbled as the words hit a dry patch in his throat. "...more than one spirit here?"

Teresa leaned forward and rested a hand on Doug's knee. It wasn't a completely reassuring gesture. More like a parent realizing her child had finally come to understand some awful truth. *Oh, you poor thing,* Doug could hear her say in his mind.

"I know this must be hard for you both," Teresa said, looking back and forth to Doug and Carla. "And I don't want you to confuse us with being exorcists or demonologists or anything of the like. However, we *will* rid this house of any negative energy here, and replace it with good, warm, positive energy. Okay?"

Doug and Carla nodded. Teresa leaned back into the sofa and said something to Alix that neither Carla nor Doug heard. Alix simply nodded and reached down into the leather satchel that rested at her feet. She opened the top flap and withdrew a folded sheet of paper. Doug couldn't see anything written on it, but for reasons unknown, he suddenly grew very uncomfortable.

"After we talked on the phone," Alix began, "I told Teresa about the goings-on in your home. I mentioned that you'd claimed to see an entity in your daughter's room. That's correct, right? It was in her room?"

Doug nodded and his body grew fidgety. He couldn't tell why, but he had a strong feeling he didn't want to see what was on the paper.

"Well," Alix continued, "Teresa, being constantly open to the spirit world, often has visions and she'll draw what she sees. Now, this may be difficult to understand, or even to see, but please know that I only told Teresa *of* an apparition; I didn't describe it to her."

"Okay," Doug said, as he glanced back and forth between Alix's eyes and the paper in her hands. He felt dizzy and winded, like the air was slowly being sucked from his lungs. It was as if no chair rested below him.

"Does this look familiar?" Alix asked.

As she unfolded the paper, the image Doug saw inspired the stuff of his nightmares. And even though it had been weeks since he'd last seen this image, he remembered it as if he'd seen it the day before or even earlier that morning. Doug recalled vividly the long dark hair, the collared shirt.

He especially remembered the black, feathered pants. It was the woman he'd seen sitting on Janie's bed.

The room started to collapse into a tunnel and his mouth formed the question before his mind was even aware he was asking it: "How?" A single tear bubbled out of one eye.

Carla turned to him. "Doug? What's wrong?" She looked at the image on the paper and then at him again. "Have you seen this woman before?"

Doug closed his eyes and inhaled slowly and deeply. He thought about the countless times he could have said something to Carla about what he saw but never did. When he saw the apparition, Carla had still been having a difficult time believing in what was really happening, so he'd kept it to himself.

He turned to her and opened his eyes. "I'm sorry I never told you," he said, almost at a whisper. His head hung with shame and another tear fell in his lap. Then he tipped his head toward the drawing in Alix's hands. "I saw that woman sitting on Janie's bed one day."

Carla brought a hand to her mouth and looked away. Doug heard her draw a sharp breath.

"I'm sorry," he said again.

Carla held back an impending waterfall and straightened. She cleared her throat. "It's okay." But Doug could clearly see it wasn't. She stared straight ahead, but not at the two mediums. And to their credit, neither Alix nor Teresa said anything. They simply allowed Carla the time to process what she'd just heard.

The guilt over never having told her about the apparition ripped through Doug's insides and he, too, fought back emotions. He sat still and watched from the corner of his eye as Carla quietly tried to figure out why he'd kept her in the dark all this time. When Doug saw her face redden with embarrassment, he wanted to throw out reason after reason as to why he acted in the way he did, but ultimately, it was a conversation best had in private.

Finally, Doug felt Carla's eyes on him and he acknowledged her. To his surprise, her face, once twisted with deception, now appeared relaxed. Genuine. She reached over and rested a hand on his. Doug found pity in Carla's face and he desperately grasped on to the smallest amount of comfort in knowing she understood why he never told her.

"I assure you," Alix said, and Doug was only too happy for the break in silence, "this is no fabrication or embellishment of our abilities."

Doug held up a hand. "I know, I know." In his eyes, the room had returned to its normal shape and the overwhelming pressure he felt moments ago began to subside. "I believe you."

"I promise," Teresa began. "I don't show you this to upset you."

"It's okay," Doug said. "I appreciate you showing me this."

"This is what I saw when Alix told me about your conversation." She glanced at the drawing and chuckled in spite of herself. "I don't claim to be any kind of artist. But drawing something like this is one way for me to connect with the people I'm trying to help."

Doug simply nodded. Though the image shocked and paralyzed him at first, he eventually realized what Teresa was trying to do. Any lingering doubt he had in this woman's abilities had long been restored.

"Would you like to know her name?" Teresa asked.

By now, he could have cried and laughed at the same time. "Are you kidding?" Doug asked.

Teresa smiled gently and shook her head, but it was Alix who spoke next.

"Her name is Rainin."

"'Raining?'"

"Almost," Alix said. "Just without the G." She said it slower the second time: "Rai-nin."

Carla reflected on this for a few seconds. "That's beautiful."

"How do you know her name?" Doug asked, then immediately assumed he knew the answer. "Did she tell you?"

"I read about her in Vera Olum's book," Teresa said. "The woman who previously lived on this land...she was a medium, too."

Doug's mouth dropped open. "You found her book?"

"Yes," Alix said. "I told you, we have resources." She winked at Doug and Carla. "The book has been out of print for over fifty years now, but I made some phone calls to friends of ours. A friend in the Midwest was able to locate the book at a local second-hand bookstore. It's actually a very short book, just a little over a hundred pages, and he was able to scan it and send us the pages in an email. Teresa was up until four this morning reading it."

"She talks a lot about her previous husband, Edgar, of course," Teresa continued. "She also wrote quite a bit about her ability to communicate with the spirits. She talks about 'Rainin,' a guardian angel she called upon frequently to watch over her and her husband, along with the children at the mission."

"She actually says that?" Doug asked. "In the book?"

Teresa nodded. "When Vera moved here," she spread her arms to indicate the home and the land on which it stood, "I believe Rainin followed her here. To protect her. To watch over the land and those who inhabit it. And when Vera passed on, Rainin stayed with the land as it was the last place Vera's soul had lived." She paused and slowly pointed a finger toward the door. "I noticed some vehicles across the street and down the road a little ways. Has the land been disturbed recently?"

"Yes," Doug said. "There have been a lot of builders lately. They started during the fall. A couple places over here were torn down and are being rebuilt. They're building a small shopping center."

Teresa nodded thoughtfully. "A disturbance in nature can often release previously inactive spirits. Spirits tend to grow accustomed to their environment. When that environment changes, it can upset them or simply make them curious. Because of the proximity to your home, and your daughter's ability to communicate, there's a very good chance they…flooded her. Overloaded her. And I think Rainin recognized this and stepped in to protect her. These spirits…they're looking for help. They don't know how to communicate; it's hard to do from the other side."

"And you believe this, too?" Carla asked Alix.

"I do," Alix confirmed. "Given the landscape, what happened here years ago, Vera's ability, and the way the land is being torn up, it's very possible Rainin felt your daughter was becoming vulnerable to the activity, and she tried to help. She's *trying* to help."

Doug clapped his hands together and pressed them against his lips. He smiled.

"She's here to help," he said, more as an affirmation to himself. Carla rubbed his back as he leaned forward and rested his elbows on his knees. A warm feeling of relief, albeit slight, cascaded through his body.

Then he remembered being shoved across Janie's room and lifted off the floor two nights ago, and the warm feeling dissipated.

"What about what happened the other night?" he asked. And then another question formed in his mind, to which he wasn't sure he wanted an answer. "And why would...why would this entity *not* like holy water?"

"Ah, yes," Teresa said. "Now that can be troubling to hear, can't it?"

Doug let out a nervous laugh. "Troubling is one way to describe it. But frankly, it kinda scared the crap out of me. I mean, of all the things in this world and beyond it, what particular being would have a negative response to holy water?" He glanced quickly at his wife. "As you can imagine, my wife and I are only able to come up with one answer."

"It's understandable," Alix said. "But we have another theory."

Doug jerked his head toward the two mediums. "You do?"

"Yes. But I think it would be best if we carry out the ceremony before we jump to any unnecessary conclusions."

Doug felt dejected, but endeavored not to let it show. "Of course, of course. Whatever you need to do."

Teresa stood and politely interjected. "Holy water can be useful...if you know what you're dealing with. However, we use an old, traditional Native American method called 'smudging,' which is done using a mixture of sage, cedar, and sweet grass. We mix them together in an abalone seashell, which symbolizes the Earth from which it came, as well as water, completing the circle of life. We then burn the mixture." She looked upward and raised her hands, simulating prayer, "And as we pray, the smoke carries our prayers to the Great Creator."

"Is that what you're going to do now?" Doug asked.

"With your permission," Teresa said, "we would be happy to bless your home with a smudging prayer. With this prayer, we believe we can remove the negative energy from your home."

Doug turned to Carla. She offered no objection, neither visibly nor verbally, and Doug couldn't think of any, either. He mused briefly at the sudden awareness that, while all this talk of spirits and smudging was new and unknown to him, he found none of it to be strange or unrealistic. Months earlier he might have found all of this to be fanciful, even resembling of some kind of voodoo. But here and now, he'd bought in to Teresa and Alix's beliefs. Their explanations were solid and true. They believed it. There was no reason for him not to.

He turned and faced the mediums once again. "How do we begin?"

Alix reached down into the leather satchel again. From it she produced a large, beautiful white abalone seashell, along with three small wooden containers. Doug thought they resembled bamboo with their round shape and stained appearance. Alix placed these on the sofa cushions and moved swiftly around the great room, opening windows.

"I know it's cold," she said, "but we'll need some ventilation in order for the smoke to carry our prayers and release the negative energy from the house. Otherwise, it can remain trapped." She continued into the kitchen, opened the sliding door a few inches, and then returned to the great room. She picked up the seashell and handed it to Teresa.

Next, she picked up one of the small wooden containers. She lifted the lid. "This is sage," she said. She removed a tightly bundled stick of dried leaves. "Sage is used to drive out negative spirits, feelings, or influences. It also prevents these kinds of spirits from entering while we perform the ceremony." She placed the sage stick into the seashell.

She reached down to the sofa cushions again and picked up the second of the three wooden containers. "This is cedar. Cedar also acts as a cleanser, removing negative energy from the home. Also, it is the cedar smoke that carries our prayers to the Great Creator."

The cedar sticks looked similar to the sage sticks, Doug noticed, as Alix placed one in the shell alongside the other herb. Doug caught Teresa's eye; she smiled peacefully back at him while Alix collected the materials.

Lastly, Alix picked up the third container. "This is sweet grass," she said.

Having never seen sweet grass before, Doug expected a similarly bundled assortment of dried leaves and herbs tied together. Instead, Alix drew back the lid and the third container revealed a beautiful braid of grass, which was green in color. The pattern looked similar to the way a young girl would braid her hair and it immediately reminded Doug of the way Carla had, on occasion, braided Janie's hair.

"Sweet grass," Alix continued, "brings in only good spirits. Also, just like cedar, we pray while the sweet grass burns and its smoke carries our prayers up to the Creator."

Alix and Teresa arranged the sage, cedar and sweet grass inside the shell. Then, Alix removed a pack of matches and an incense stick from her pocket.

"Now we light them," Alix said, "but we don't want to create a flame. The trick is to get it to smolder, which is what I'll use this for." She held up the incense.

Alix proceeded to light the end of the incense and waited until the tip achieved a bright red-orange glow. Then she inserted the stick below the leaves inside the shell. She blew softly into the smudge mixture so as not to create a flame and only to produce a light smoke.

Teresa closely analyzed the herbal mixture in the seashell. "I think I see something."

"Yep," Alix agreed. "We're almost there."

Doug and Carla exchanged a guarded glance and Doug felt doubt crawling in once again—doubt in Alix and Teresa; doubt in the ceremony's effectiveness. But he also knew most actions, such as the one taking place in front of him and Carla, required a healthy amount of faith in order to work. A strong belief. Doug's belief in the entities haunting his home had been secured long before the two mediums arrived in his home. He wasn't sure why he was so hesitant to believe in Teresa and Alix's methods. After all, they seemed genuine, as if they'd done this a thousand times before.

"First," Alix said, cutting into Doug's thoughts, "we will smudge ourselves."

By now the smoke that rose from the shell, while not quite billowing, was thick enough that Doug could see and smell it. The sage and sweet grass together produced an earthy, pungent odor Doug could nearly taste on his tongue, while the strong and sweet air of the cedar filled their immediate space.

Then Teresa began to pray: "Angel Gabriel on my left, Angel Michael on my right, may you please protect and surround us with love and light."

Alix pushed the smoke with open hands against and around Teresa, as if wrapping the older medium in the burnt offering, while Teresa repeated the prayer over and over. When Alix was done, Teresa walked around using her own hand to brush the smoke against Alix while she continued reciting the prayer.

When she was done smudging Alix, Teresa walked to Carla and Doug and repeated the same process. As she recited the prayer over and over, Doug thought this might be a queue for him and Carla to follow. At one point, he caught Alix's eyes; he notched his eyebrows quickly, his own eyes darting to Teresa and then back to Alix as if to ask, "Should we join?" Alix smiled and quietly offered a reassuring shake of her head. It was fine, Doug thought. They were in Teresa's hands now. She would pray for all of them.

After several minutes of smudging, the elder medium moved to the main door to the house and continued her prayer. Alix followed her and waved Carla and Doug over, beckoning them to stand closer to her and Teresa.

Doug and Carla walked toward Teresa and stopped just behind her. The smoke field was now very thick, much thicker than when they had begun. It spread as they moved from the center of the great room to the front door.

At first, Doug attempted to breathe into his sleeve when the smoky mixture started to itch his throat, but after a while, he felt a peace fall over him; it was a pacification that made his body feel lighter than its 180 pounds. Even his head felt lighter and his eyelids felt heavier, but not to the extent he felt sleepy. Rather, his mind, body, and soul were incredibly relaxed. Any strain and tension that once occupied his muscles was now gone. He thought he might float through the entire house just then, but he realized this could simply be an effect created by the smudging process.

With the smudging completed in the great room, the four of them moved into the kitchen. Again, Teresa called out to the Angels Michael and Gabriel, and even the Great Creator, and she asked them to protect the house with love and light. Doug closed his eyes and saw only darkness. Then, while concentrating on Teresa's prayers, an image began to materialize in the black.

It was Janie. She wore a two-piece pajama set and held a doll in one arm.

J-Bird, Sweetie...

In his mind's eye, Doug saw her smile. She looked innocent and calm. Nobody could harm her now. Nobody and nothing. When this was over, she'd be able to come home and sleep in her own bed. *Heck*, Doug thought, *I might just drive over to Luke and Diane's and bring her back home tonight.*

As he watched Janie in silent adoration for the courage she had shown the past several months, and as he listened to the mediums' prayer, a third voice entered his ears. Teresa and Alix weren't the only voices in the room anymore. His eyelids opened gently as if pulled up by tiny, helium-filled balloons. To his left, Carla had joined the prayer. Doug considered nudging her, or possibly grabbing her hand, but the intensity in her face prevented him from breaking her focus.

When they finished smudging around the sliding door and windows of the kitchen, they proceeded to the rest of the house. They smudged every open space: every doorway, closet, window. Doug hadn't noticed it until now, but Teresa had removed a small vial of oil from her pocket. For each new opening they smudged, she would draw a cross at the top of each one with an oiled fingertip. Alix explained that every doorway or opening to the house could act as a portal through which the spirits could enter, so it was important that special attention be paid to every opening.

When they reached Janie's room, Doug felt a cold breeze as they walked over the threshold.

Teresa stopped in the center of the room and hesitated before continuing the prayer. Doug studied her as she patiently surveyed the room.

"This will take some time," she finally said. It was the first moment since they'd begun the ceremony that Doug's peace had been interrupted. He'd felt 'one with the Creator' ever since the smudge-smoke took its hold on him.

Until now.

Teresa appeared to meditate to herself, speaking so inaudibly that neither Doug nor Carla could hear. Alix, who had been at her side through the entire ceremony, stepped away to be with Doug and Carla.

"This may be hard to watch," Alix told them. Her voice was low, but her tone wasn't reassuring like before. This time it was grave. "Surprisingly, it's been a fairly smooth process so far. But there's definitely a presence here, and it doesn't want to leave."

Doug and Carla had no response and only nodded.

"You may see her do something...unexpected," Alix tried to explain. "But whatever it is, do *not* try to stop her, under any circumstances. Understand? Do not try to interfere. Do not try to help. Even if she touches you in any way...do not interrupt. This is very critical."

"Okay," Carla murmured.

Doug shot her a look of awe. There was hardly a trace of hesitation or worry in her voice. Her trust and confidence filled him with pride. She was incredibly strong and he had to bury a sudden emotional uprising in his chest.

Alix walked over to Janie's window and tried to open it. She struggled at first; even when she lowered herself for a bit more leverage, Doug noticed the pane didn't shake or bang in the way a stubborn window often does when it refuses to slide up its track.

"They don't want you to open it," Teresa warned. Her voice then rose with surprising command: "You have to fight them!" Carla flinched at the abrupt change in her tone. "Fight them!" Teresa demanded again.

Doug felt an involuntary movement in his leg; he wanted to help, but he remembered what Alix had said only moments ago...

It was nearly impossible for him not to try to help. Every modern convention about gender told him to help. His very constitution implored him to go to the window to assist Alix. But spiritually, he knew he was in way over his head. This was beyond his understanding. The window wasn't simply stuck. This wasn't the same as helping Carla open the jelly jar because the crystallized sugar had created a bond too tight for her to break. The window's bonds were held in place by another force...something unnatural and not of the normal world.

"You must open it!" Teresa called out again.

Doug heard a helpless groan escape from Alix's gritted teeth as she bent beneath the sill and pushed upward against the bottom rail. Then, a slight creak of wood against wood. The sash ached as it finally slid upwards in a stuttering motion. After what felt like hours and what was likely only a few seconds, there were a few inches of open space between the rail and the sill. Alix, physically exhausted—and mentally, Doug thought—backed away and stood next to Teresa who continued with the prayer.

Together, the two mediums moved toward the closet and continued the smudging process, passing the sage/cedar/sweet grass mixture along the entire closet frame, and then the window, before finally coming back to the center of the bedroom.

"Oh, Great One!" Teresa cried out, her head tilted toward the sky. "Be with me now! Guide me as I cleanse this home of all this negative energy!"

At once, her head jerked and her attention turned to the corner of the room—the space between Janie's closet and the rocking chair. Doug squinted to see what she was staring at, but he saw nothing.

"Do you see them?" Teresa called out. "Do you see them there?"

Foolishly, Doug nearly replied with a no, but was cut off by Alix before he could speak.

"I see them!" Alix said.

Together, Teresa and Alix moved toward the space in the corner. Teresa held the smudging shell in front of her body, fanning the smoke in a circular motion.

"You are not wanted here!" Teresa yelled toward the corner of the room. Then she turned to Alix and said much more quietly, "We need a candle."

Alix left the room immediately. Teresa continued to stare into the corner, channeling all of her energy toward that space. She remained silent, as if tracking something invisible to Doug's and Carla's eyes.

Seconds later, Alix returned with a short, round white candle. She struck a match against the matchbook and lit the wick. She then placed the candle on the windowsill and remained there.

"You are looking for help!" Teresa continued. "But we are not able to help you!" Without taking her eyes off the thing in the corner of the room, Teresa moved to the window. She gestured toward the candle. "You need to find the light! This is where you will find your answers!"

"We cannot help you!" Alix exclaimed, finally joining the verbal commands being shouted. She gestured a hand through the open window and out into the night air. "You must leave! You are not wanted here!"

Without warning, the window came crashing down its track with full force, crushing Alix's hand. She yelped and collapsed to her knees under the pain, grabbing onto the wrist of her pinned hand. Teresa halted the ceremony and raced toward Alix; she worked feverishly to raise the window.

Stunned, Doug winced in horror at Alix's pained expression. He remembered what she'd said about not helping, but sensed this warranted his assistance. When he felt Carla's elbow jab him in the side, he spoke up.

"Please, can I help?"

"Yes," Teresa managed to say as she struggled against the window.

Doug was quickly next to Teresa and together, he and the older medium worked to pry the window off Alix's hand. He was immediately shocked by the force that worked against them, as if ten men were on the other side, holding down the window. At once he lowered himself, just as Alix had done initially, and leaned upward against the bottom rail. Slowly, the window opened and Alix quickly removed her hand. It was too dark for him to see how badly her hand had been damaged internally, but he saw blood begin to gush from an open wound and motioned for Carla to help.

"Grab a towel!" he said. "And some ice!"

Carla ran from the room as Teresa and Doug aided Alix, who leaned against the wall.

"It might be broken," she said.

"That's fine," Teresa said. "We'll get you to a hospital after. If we need to."

"After?" Doug asked incredulously.

"Yes," Teresa insisted. "After. We are too far into the ceremony. If we stop now, it'll only make things worse."

Doug spread his hands out. "But she might have a broken hand for god's sake! She needs medical attention!"

"She's right," Alix said, supporting herself with her good hand as she began to rise from the floor.

Carla entered the room again and wrapped a small towel around Alix's hand. "There's a bag of ice wrapped inside the towel," she said. "That should help with the swelling."

"Thank you," Alix said, and turned back to Doug. "And Teresa's right. If we stop now, it can only get much worse. We have to continue."

"You're going to continue?" Carla asked. She was just as puzzled as Doug.

Teresa placed a reassuring hand on Carla's arm. "You must trust us. We've seen this kind of thing many times before. We understand the risks."

Carla looked over to Alix with a concerned expression.

"It's true," Alix confirmed. "We know there's always a chance one of us could get hurt. What's important now is that we press on. If my hand is broken, it'll still be broken when I get to the hospital."

Carla stared at her in awe. Doug was equally impressed by Alix's resolve. In his mind, he still had one foot out the door, hand on the wheel, key in the ignition...but it wasn't his call. Not now.

He finally relented. "Okay then," he said steadily. "Let's move on."

At that, Teresa hurried back to the corner of the room. Alix slowly followed her.

The older medium stared into the corner a few moments, then lashed out an arm and swung at something neither Doug nor Carla could see.

"Get out!" she yelled. She swung again. "You are not wanted here!" She turned her head skyward. "Oh, Great Creator! Help these lost souls to find the light! Show them the light! Make them feel its warmth and energy! Tell them their place is not here!"

"Help us, Great One!" Alix cried. "Be with us! Guide these lost souls toward the light!"

"Their spirit is strong," Teresa begged, "but you are stronger, Great One! Help them! Help them find the light!"

As the two mediums worked tirelessly, Doug's emotions erupted. There was a moment before it happened when he tried to hold it back, but it was like trying to dam a body of water with only twigs. His tears came not slow and steady, but as a geyser, gushing over his cheeks and down to the floor as he watched the two mediums, two grown women, struggle against this entity. Doug could only imagine the conflict his daughter had endured all this time. Her constant acting-out and misbehavior was likely the result of some internal, several-months-long strife; a combination of everything she'd gone through, compartmentalized and redirected at Doug and Carla with full force. The cold, helpless feeling of not having known until now overcame him. Grief poured out in salty, candle-shimmering rivers of heartbreak.

Suddenly, Teresa stopped. Alix stopped, too. Doug choked back his sobs; for a moment, he thought it was over.

The ceremony was finished and their house was theirs once again. All was finally about to return back to normal.

Then Teresa turned to him and Carla, and the intensity in her eyes told him it was far from over.

"We need to be outside," Teresa told him.

Doug forced the lump in his throat down into his stomach and was able to speak. "Sure," he said. "We can go now. Should we—"

"No," Teresa cut him off. *"We"*—she waved a hand between herself and Alix—"need to go outside. You and Carla will have to stay inside for the remainder."

"Okay."

Doug was hardly upset by this change in tact. He wasn't happy, either, but he accepted their wishes with indifference. He didn't ask why he and Carla couldn't join them outside. He only moved out of the way to let Teresa and Alix by as they left Janie's room and walked into the hallway.

"Right now," Alix said as they walked, "we're going to continue with the smudging outside. It's important to perform the ceremony in the yard as well."

Carla stared at Alix's hand. The younger medium held the dressings securely around the wound. There was a lot of blood.

"Are you sure we can't help?" Carla asked.

Alix stopped. A sympathetic smile traced her lips. "You've both done so well tonight. But for what happens next, we need to do it alone."

Carla nodded.

Doug motioned toward the front door in the great room. "Well," he said, "you can either go out the front, or use the sliding doors to the backyard."

"We'll begin out front," Teresa said.

With that, the two mediums exited the front door.

Doug and Carla stood quietly in the great room and watched from their bay window. Teresa and Alix moved to the perimeter of the property, starting with the end of the driveway, and continued in the same manner of moving the smoke from the seashell in large circular motions. Naturally, Doug couldn't hear what was being said, but he expected the prayer to be the same and he began to say the words over and over in his head, as if by doing so the ceremony would have a greater chance of success.

After ten minutes of watching in silence, Doug lamented, "I wonder why we can't be with them?"

Carla backed away and let out an exhausted breath. The night's events had finally taken their toll on her, physically and mentally, and she fell backward into the couch cushions. "I don't think it's for us to understand," she sighed.

Doug continued to watch in earnest as the mediums proceeded up the side of the yard, craning at an awkward angle until they were no longer in view.

"They're headed out back," he said.

Carla let out a muffled, "Mm," as Doug moved quickly past the couch, stepped over her legs, and raced into the kitchen.

Their participation having been suspended for the remainder of the smudging, Doug's adrenaline still raged. "Why we can't help?" he asked again with more frustration.

This time, Carla said nothing in response. She remained slouched on the couch and nearly flattened. Her eyes were closed.

"We live here," Doug continued. "You'd think they would need the homeowners for this entire... thing."

He watched from the sliding doors as the mediums performed their ritual throughout the backyard. They moved along the fence that bordered Esther's yard in seemingly planned intervals and then continued toward the tree line that stretched from Esther's to Wayne's properties. When they reached the trees, they stopped.

Doug watched as they took turns pointing and gesturing toward certain parts of the woods. They hadn't done this at any other point in the ceremony. Doug knew there was a stream back there that ran parallel to the road, but his property ended before it.

After some discussion that Doug could not hear, Alix walked into the trees and disappeared into the dark.

"She just took off into the woods," Doug said.

"Hm?" Carla murmured.

"Alix. She just walked out into the trees. Where the heck is she going?"

Carla patted a weary hand against the couch cushion. "Come sit down, babe. I'm sure they know what they're doing."

Doug entertained Carla's offer with only lukewarm interest. He wanted to see what they were doing. He *needed* to see. He stared out into the inky abyss beyond the trees. He paid no attention to Teresa who did the same, her back toward the house.

His finger on the door handle, Doug was about to slide the door open when Alix reappeared. There was some more discussion between her and Teresa, then a continuation of the ceremony, and then finally, the two mediums moved away from the tree line and up the hedgerow that bordered Wayne's property. Doug backed away from the door and folded his arms. By now, another hour had passed and the rush Doug once felt had finally subsided. The ceremony outside appeared to be anything but eventful.

That's probably why they didn't need us, he thought.

Doug's nerves had long since leveled off when he saw Teresa and Alix walking through the middle of the backyard and toward the house.

So that's it, he thought. *It's done. We can have our house back.*

When the mediums were fifteen feet from the sliding doors, Teresa stopped abruptly. She grabbed Alix's arm. Her eyes went wide and she doubled over, as if punched in the stomach. Doug stopped breathing as he watched Alix try to speak to Teresa. The older medium was unresponsive.

Doug reached down for the door handle without looking and swatted at only empty space. His eyes finally followed his hands and he located the handle. He grabbed it with both hands and yanked the door away from the jamb.

When he looked back at where the mediums had been standing, they were gone. His eyes darted around and he quickly found both women rushing toward the side of the house.

Doug closed the door, ran back into the great room and tracked them from several windows. Teresa was fine — clearly her sudden attack was not of the medical kind — and Alix tried to keep up with the older medium as Teresa raced toward the chimney.

Doug turned to Carla, who was still resting on the couch. "They're back!"

Carla, whose eyes had rested emptily on the ceiling over the last hour, finally snapped to attention. "What? Where?"

Doug had already turned back to the window. "They were coming back in. I thought they were done. And then something happened to Teresa and they both ran over to the chimney."

"What?" Carla asked as she rose from the couch. She moved quickly toward the window.

"Look!" Doug said, pointing outside.

Teresa leaned against the chimney; she supported herself with one hand while holding the seashell in the other. Her head moved up and down, concentrating on the ground, and then up at the sky. Doug could see her lips moving. He could even faintly hear her speak. She was commanding the spirit to leave, much how she had in Janie's room.

Alix was there, too, holding Teresa with her good hand, as if steadying the old woman to keep her from falling. They both called upon the Great One, the Great Creator, and asked him to release the "troubled" spirit.

Doug couldn't tell for sure, but it sounded like they had located an entity different from those they had found in Janie's room. He shot a look of concern at Carla. She didn't acknowledge him and only continued to stare out the window.

Doug looked out again. Teresa no longer leaned against the chimney. Now she stood completely upright, her arms out wide, one hand on the shell, one hand open. Alix worked rapidly but methodically, carefully controlling the smoke that rose from the smudge shell and moving it around the two of them. As she worked with haste, she continued her incantations, but Doug was unable to hear her above Teresa's prayers.

Then Alix stopped. She backed away from Teresa. Doug pressed his face against the glass; his breath had fogged up the window and he wiped away the moisture that obscured his view. The old woman appeared stunned, frozen in place. Her arms remained out at her sides, but she seemed stuck there, unable to move.

"What the—" Doug began to say, but he was unable to find any appropriate words. He stared at the old medium. His heart pounded and he watched as Teresa's eyes called upon the heavens. Her body quivered as if the winds of a small tornado twisted around her. To Doug, she appeared possessed.

To his shock, Alix simply stood by. However, neither her visage nor her body showed apathy or a lack of readiness. She remained cautious and astute, patient and prepared, revealing a truth that left Doug even more confounded: Alix had seen this before.

"Why isn't she—" Carla started to ask, but Doug quieted her with a single raised finger. Carla was smart. She would likely put it together on her own. Now was not a time to discuss. Doug only wanted to watch in silence and send his prayers to the Great Creator, through Alix and Teresa.

THIS is why they wanted us to stay inside.

Doug watched in wonder as the mediums channeled their collective energy to bring peace to the spirits, to help them find the light. While inside, Doug felt a light burn within his stomach; it was a warm, soothing gel that spread into his chest and forced out the anxiety that had resided there the past couple months. In a way, he felt his own spirit lifted. His shoulders were weightless, his feet like feathers. He could hardly feel the ground as his soul was healed of its wounds and…reborn.

He looked over to Carla, who still watched from the other window. She caught his stare and returned it. Her eyes and cheeks were wet. She smiled. Doug smiled back and reached out his hand. She took it and moved into him. She wrapped her arms around him, rested her head against his chest, and they both stared outside at the scene happening by their chimney. Doug didn't recall if he'd ever mentioned to Alix the things about the coal stove, how it apparently "fed" itself during the night, but it didn't matter. The feeling in his heart that was once dread and despair had been chased away and replaced by hope.

After an eternity, Teresa's arms began to fall slowly and steadily until they relaxed at her sides. She stood and stared at the ground a while. Her lips moved gently, likely in prayer, Doug thought. Amazingly, she still held the seashell. She never dropped it once.

After a few minutes of quiet prayer, Alix stepped closer and put an arm on Teresa's shoulder. Doug could now hear the two of them, but their prayers barely reached a mumble, their words unclear and indecipherable. Alix turned toward the window, toward Doug. She knew he and Carla had been watching the whole time. She simply nodded. A sincere and direct gesture that meant only one thing: You're safe now. They were all safe. The ceremony was finished. *It was over.*

CHAPTER 28

When they came back inside the house, the two mediums sat down on the sofa in the great room. Neither spoke for a while. The only communication between them and Doug and Carla consisted mostly of small hand and head gestures and some half-questions: "Could I...?" "Would you...?" When Carla served tea again, Alix and Teresa kindly accepted without words.

Teresa's appearance was that of someone who'd just run a marathon—perspiration on her face, hair tangled and messy, her head and shoulders hanging with fatigue. She sank into the cushions of the sofa and rested.

Alix sat quietly as well. Both her hands rested in her lap. Doug noticed she didn't seem uncomfortable at that moment, but he was still concerned about her injured hand. Alix had indicated the swelling was going down and she was able to make a fist without much discomfort. He offered to drive her to the hospital just in case, but she politely declined.

Afterward, the group sat in complete silence, sipping tea and water. Ultimately, it was Alix who would first reflect on what had taken place. She shared that reflection with Doug and Carla.

Alix explained that a spirit had tried very hard to communicate with Teresa and, in doing so, "grabbed" her and wouldn't let her leave until she'd understood.

"He was young," Alix said of the spirit that occupied the space near the chimney. "Probably fifteen or sixteen years old. And he was certainly Native American."

"How do you know that?" Doug asked.

"A few hundred years ago this land would have been heavily populated by local Native Americans, even Native Canadians." She pointed toward the glass doors. "Are you familiar with the stream back there?"

Doug knew she was referring to the brook out in the woods just beyond his property line.

"Yes," said Doug. "We've been back there before. Not very often though. I'm a little nervous about spending time back there. You know, because of my daughter...I'm not sure if there's poison ivy back there or what. I don't go back there often."

"Well," Alix continued, "I'm not sure if you're aware of this, but that stream runs for quite a few miles and empties out into Congamond Lake."

She had referred to the popular summer destination for fishermen, boaters and swimmers. Doug was very familiar with the lake as it sat on the Massachusetts/Connecticut border, only a few miles from their home.

"It's very likely," Alix said, "that natives would have traveled by way of this stream down to the lake, which would have served as a great source of water and food. In essence, it's quite possible that the natives lived off this very land.

"Earlier today," Alix continued, "we took a look at a map of your town, including your exact address. Given the location, the tree line, and the proximity of the water source, this land would have offered a great opportunity for hunting, fishing, shelter, you name it.

"Wow," Doug said, highly impressed with Alix's knowledge of the land. "Did you study Native American history or something?"

Even as he asked the question, the answer came to him. Surprisingly, it was the first time all night that Doug had taken notice of Alix's straight black hair, high cheekbones, and darker complexion.

"I'm Native American." Alix said. "I'm originally from South Dakota, but I live in Connecticut now. I still have a lot of family out west, but to answer your question, yes, I did study Native American culture quite extensively. And, I can also tell you that Native Americans didn't use holy water during prayer or blessing. They used oils, herbs, and other natural substances. Since they wouldn't have been introduced to holy water until the Europeans arrived, the concept would have been an altogether foreign one."

Lights began to turn on in Doug's head, illuminating the shadows in the darkest parts of his mind. Everything Alix was saying was plausible. If the spirit that pushed him was Native American, then it was reasonable to believe it had no idea what kind of water Doug had used to bless the house. It was just as possible the spirit didn't recognize the blessing at all and assumed Doug was trying to attack it. But all this explanation still begged yet another question.

"Janie called him 'Mr. Achak,'" Doug said. "Is 'Achak' a Native American name?"

At this point, even Alix was impressed. "Wow. That sounds Algonquin. And the Algonquin tribe was definitely in this area."

"Why is—" Carla started to ask, but then restated her question. "Why *was* he here? The Native American boy?"

"He didn't have a choice," Alix said. "He was...I guess the best way to describe it is that he was forced to stay here."

"Forced?" Doug asked. "Like he was trapped or something? Had he been pinned under a rock or something like that?"

At this point, Teresa had apparently regained enough strength and she joined the conversation.

"He was meant to stay," Teresa said. "I could hear him. I could feel him. He didn't want to be here, but he was unable to leave, at least not on his own." She began to massage her wrists, alternating between her right and left. "His hands and feet had been bound and I could feel it."

"You think someone tied him up and left him?" Doug asked.

Teresa nodded.

"Why would someone want to do that?"

"This was a long time ago," Teresa said. "And as we mentioned before, that stream in your back yard dumps into a large body of water a few miles from here. The natives likely passed by this land many times." Her eyes looked off as she recalled the event outside. "There was definitely a struggle. A struggle over the land." She gestured toward the back yard. "Likely over this very part of the stream. It's possible there was a village here and it was attacked, perhaps by another tribe."

Doug thought about this for a moment. He listened to Teresa's words a couple more times in his head. There was something that bothered him, something he wanted to ask. He turned to Carla. The strain on her brow told him she had the same question.

"Is he gone?" Doug asked. "Is the boy gone? Or will he stay here?"

"He is gone," Teresa said. "I helped him to find the light. The others wouldn't let him go. That's when Rainin tried to help him. And when she did, the others didn't like it."

"Others?" Doug asked.

"The other spirits," Teresa said. "That's why they lashed out at you and your family. Rainin's first obligation was to the boy. When the others became angry, they went after Janie as she was most vulnerable. And then, the whole family."

"That's why Janie was never hurt by it," he realized.

Teresa nodded. "Rainin tried to protect all of you, but it became too much for her. She couldn't help the boy *and* protect your daughter *and* protect the family. It was just too difficult. She couldn't protect you against all of them. Ultimately, there was too much negative energy here and she was losing."

Carla leaned forward. "Wait a minute. What about the sheets being pulled off the bed, the bed shaking, Janie complaining about the lights? Who did all that?"

"It was most likely Achak," Teresa said. "The good spirit trying to get your attention. None of those things were truly malicious acts. He, too, was probably aware that Rainin was struggling, and those events were likely his way of reaching out for help."

"And what about the stove?" Doug asked.

Teresa looked at him curiously, then turned to Alix. She also had no answer.

"What stove?" Alix asked.

"Sorry," Doug said, "I never explained that. In the beginning, months ago, we had heard someone shoveling coal into the stove at night." He nodded toward the coal stove. "How would a Native American have any idea how to operate it?"

Alix studied the stove and considered Doug's question before asking, "Was the stove already burning when you heard the activity?"

"Yes."

Alix nodded. "Then think of it this way: Native Americans were very competent at creating fire, and even more so at sustaining it. To him, it wasn't that he understood how to operate the stove, but he would have easily understood that the coal simply represented the fuel required by the fire to remain ignited. And, since that particular area is the space that confined him, we can assume he was cold and needed warmth."

"Okay, wait a minute," Carla interjected. "If this person was Native American, how would Janie have been able to communicate with him? How would a Native American spirit have known how to speak English?"

"Right," Alix began, "and I should have clarified. The spirit Teresa helped outside by your chimney was certainly

Native American. However, there were many spirits here, and it's possible not *all* of them were Native American."

Damn, Doug thought.

"So then, who was Janie speaking to?" Carla asked.

Alix shrugged. "It's possible that the spirit communicating with your daughter was using the 'Achak' name as a ruse, a way of concealing its true identity."

Carla inhaled deeply. "Oh boy…"

Alix laughed. "It's okay, I assure you. Whoever it was, they're gone now."

"They're all gone, dear," Teresa confirmed. "There's no bad energy here anymore."

Doug wrapped an arm around his wife and held her close. He met both mediums' eyes and thanked them with a silent nod.

"When we started," Teresa began to say, "I told you we would rid the house of the negative energy and replace it with only good, positive energy. Right? Well, the negative energy that was responsible for harming your family is gone now."

"What about Rainin?" Carla stammered.

"She is still here," Alix said. "She's here to protect your daughter from any negative energy from the spirit world."

"Will she stay here?" Carla asked.

Teresa leaned forward and placed a warm hand over Carla's. "There's only good energy here now," she said. "Rainin is good. She means your family no harm. Of course, if you want, you can ask her to leave and she will."

Carla turned to Doug. Even as she studied his eyes, Doug was already nodding his head.

"I think it's okay if she stays," Carla said.

Doug turned to Teresa. "Please tell her we say 'thank you.'"

"Why don't you tell her yourself?" Teresa asked with a smile.

Such a notion was both empowering and humbling. Even though Doug had shouted at the spirit in Janie's room only two nights ago, he never actually considered "speaking" with one. However, it was nice to know someone on the other side would be listening.

"She can hear you," Teresa reassured him. "Even if you can't hear her."

CHAPTER 29

Minutes after the mediums left their home, Doug and Carla drove over to Luke and Diane's to pick up Janie. It was late, past ten o'clock, but Doug had sent his brother a text message asking if they were still awake. To Doug's surprise, his cell phone buzzed almost immediately. Luke and Diane were still awake. The kids were up, too. None of them had wanted to go to sleep without knowing if the spirits were gone.

When Doug and Carla came up the walkway to Luke and Diane's house, Janie burst through her aunt and uncle's front door, ran to her father and threw her arms around him. She was already dressed in her footie pajamas. Doug's heart gushed when she yelled, "Daddy!" and he picked her up and held her tightly, as if for the first time. Like the day she was born. Her brown hair clung to his beard stubble and tickled his nose.

And when she asked if Mr. Achak was gone, Doug told her, "He found his way home, Sweetie."

Doug and Carla thanked Diane for recommending Teresa and Alix. It was an experience neither of them would ever forget. When Doug asked Diane, again, how the two mediums had helped her in the past, Diane coyly promised to tell him...some *other* time. The night had already been long enough, and they all needed their rest.

After a few hugs and several words of thanks, Doug, Carla and Janie went home.

Janie didn't sleep in her parents' bed that night; she slept in her own room, instead. In her own bed. She didn't wake up until long after the sun had risen above the horizon, after its warm fingers reached through the blinds and caressed her face and assured her that today would be different. There would be more happiness today than yesterday or any of the days before it.

Doug and Carla slept long and peacefully.

The following night, Doug, Carla and Janie walked out into their backyard, past the tree line and into the woods. When they came upon the stream, Doug produced a small quantity of sage, cedar and sweet grass. Teresa and Alix had left some at their home and instructed Doug and Carla on how to use it for maintenance purposes. It was Doug's idea to bring Janie down to the stream, light the mixture as the mediums had done, and allow Janie to say her own prayer.

"What do I say, Daddy?" she asked him.

"Just say what's in your heart, J-Bird."

Her nose wrinkled and her lips moved to one side of her mouth. She looked to Carla for assistance.

"It's okay, Sweetie," Carla assured her. "We know Mr. Achak was your friend and we just want you to be able to say goodbye in your own way."

"Goodbye?" she asked. "But I thought Mr. Achak was already gone?"

Doug squatted down at eye level with his daughter. "He is, honey, but he can still hear you. Right, Mommy?"

"That's right," Carla said. "See, Janie? So if there's anything you want to say, just go ahead. You can say it out loud or to yourself."

"How will he hear me?" Janie asked.

Doug held out the herb mixture — he'd arranged it on a large piece of tree bark — and showed it to her.

"See this?" he asked. "It's a very special kind of ingredient." He lit the mixture until it produced a light smoke. "It burns very slowly and the smoke carries your prayers to Mr. Achak."

"How?" Janie asked.

Doug's eyes widened. "Magic."

Janie's eyes became large and she mouthed the word, "Wow."

"So if there's something you want to tell him," Doug continued "he'll hear you."

Janie stared into his eyes and searched for any untruths Doug wasn't telling her. In fact, he wasn't lying to her, but merely stretching the truth.

Ultimately, it worked. Janie took the piece of bark from Doug's outstretched hand, then turned and walked closer to the stream.

"Okay," she said. "I'm going to say goodbye quietly."

"That's fine, Sweetie," Carla said. "If you want us to wait at home, we can do that. Or, we can stay right here. It's your call."

"I want you to wait here," she said, keeping her back to them.

"You got it, J-Bird," Doug said. "We'll be right here."

He watched Janie first bow her head before looking up into the sky and, in that moment, Doug watched his daughter grow up. Once again she took another step toward becoming a young woman, somewhat similar to the steps she'd taken in the past, but also different. She was no longer the same child she'd been only days earlier. She had matured a lot and understood the world better than she had before. Doug watched Carla watching Janie and knew she'd realized it too. He felt an enormous pride, but also sorrow: it was one more of life's lessons he would never be able to teach Janie again.

When she was finished, Janie turned and faced her parents.

"Okay," she said. "I'm done praying now."

"How do you feel?" Carla asked.

Janie's eyes looked around as she considered the question. Then, her face dropped a little.

"I feel sad."

"That's okay," Doug told her. "It's all right to feel sad."

She walked closer to Doug and Carla. Doug again dropped down at eye-level with Janie.

"I just hope he hears me," Janie said as she handed back the piece of bark.

"He heard you, Sweetie," Doug assured her. "He heard every word you said. Promise."

Janie looked into his eyes as he smiled, then up at Carla. Carla rested a hand on Janie's shoulder.

"That's our brave girl," Carla said.

Janie giggled and looked back at Doug. She reached her arms around his neck and hugged him.

"Thank you, Daddy."

Doug squeezed her gently. "You're welcome, Sweetie."

When Janie let go, Carla stepped around her and said, "Okay, who wants to race me back to the door!"

"I do!" Janie shouted.

The two of them darted through the trees and back toward the house. Doug fell behind them and walked out.

As he did, he looked up and said a silent prayer, asked the angels to watch over Achak now that he was with them. Then he walked out of the woods.

EPILOGUE

In the weeks that followed, the Mitchell house had returned to a state of normalcy. Doors no longer opened and slammed shut on their own, bottles of soda stopped projecting from the fridge, the stove burned only as brightly and as long as was allowed by the amount of coal Doug had placed inside at the end of the night.

Janie's grades improved immediately and her overall disposition returned to normal. Doug also managed to repair his relationship with Janie's teacher, Linda Trout. The next time he met with her, he apologized for his behavior during their previous meeting. Ms. Trout assured him it was quite all right and that she might have reacted the same had it been her own child.

Margaret Thompson ended up keeping Carla as Nicholas' caregiver. She never once asked again about the ghost and she never mentioned a word to any of the other parents. Carla didn't say anything about the meeting with Teresa and Alix, or the ceremony, and continued her interactions with Margaret and the rest of the parent-base as if nothing had happened.

One night, before going to sleep, Diane went into Caleb's room and checked on him. He was sound asleep on his back, arms up and out at his sides like a football referee signaling a field goal. She ran her fingers along the soft, chubby skin of his face.

She smiled at the memory of Janie running into Doug's arms the night he and Carla had come over after the mediums' ceremony. As soon as he'd entered the house, she immediately sensed a weight had been lifted from his shoulders. His face, once taut and full of worry, had been relaxed and empty of trepidation. As a mother, she very much understood a parent's love and how Doug would have done anything to protect his daughter. She was simply happy and honored to have been able to provide any assistance, even if it was only in the form of Alix's phone number.

As she left Caleb's room, she looked one last time at him sleeping in his crib. She closed her eyes, stood for a moment, and listened to his soft breathing. She revered his innocence and said a silent prayer to preserve it for as long as possible. She then turned, pulled the door closed as she walked out, and went to bed.

The spirit known as "Mr. Achak" sat in the glider in Caleb's room and began to rock.

AUTHOR'S NOTE

A long time ago, before I ever began writing my first novel, I read an interview with Stephen King in which he said every horror writer should have a good haunted house story. Even before I became a writer, that notion struck me somewhere deep. After all, it makes sense. Any time you can turn a safe haven into the scariest place on earth, people will respond. Nobody wants to live in a truly haunted home. Any time you see a shadow pass by in the living room, or you swear you heard your name called out in a whisper just as you are about to fall asleep, you know it's only your mind playing tricks on you.

But what if it's not?

Someone close to me first told me about his family's experience with the paranormal several years ago. At the time, I was still finishing up edits for my first book, *Dead Summit*, and working on Eileen Dietz's biography. However, the more he told me about his experiences, the more I became fascinated and the more I needed to know. It wasn't long before I knew I had to turn his family's story into a book. So, with his family's blessing, I set out to do so as earnestly and as truthfully as I could.

While this is a work of fiction and all names have been changed, Doug, Carla, Janie, Diane, Teresa, Alix, Vera, and Edgar are *real* people.

Teresa and Alix are real working mediums who provided guidance to Doug and Carla when nobody else would. They neither asked for, nor accepted, any money for their time and assistance. Doug and Carla swear by their gifts and have not had any experiences like those described herein since the mediums' visit. The explanation they provide in the book is the same provided by the real Teresa and Alix. Teresa's drawing of Rainin also exists exactly as described in *Those Among Us*.

Vera and Edgar Olum are real people who long ago passed on from this life. They were an extraordinary couple who performed missionary work in the country of Sumatra. The book, *O Bok Su*, written by Edgar's real-life widow, also exists.

Diane is also a real person, and although she is not Doug's real-life sister-in-law, she is family, and offered spiritual advice on more than one occasion.

Doug does *not* work in a call center, but I assure you he is a real person and he is my family. Carla is, too, and she *does* operate a daycare out of their home. Since the smudging, none of the daycare children have expressed any concern about anything paranormal.

Janie is the coolest and toughest nine-year-old girl I have ever met. She is also my family. The majority of the activity took place when she was between six and seven years old. How she managed to deal with all of this at such a young age I will never understand, but will forever admire. I cannot thank Janie or her family enough for their assistance with this book and for allowing me to share their story with you, the reader.

Janie still keeps "contact" with the other side to this day.

Invariably, I will get asked about my own personal experiences with the paranormal. In fact, before this book was printed, I was asked several times about my experiences. And whether it was by sheer coincidence or some unseen force, several things did happen.

One morning, as I was getting ready to leave for work, our TV turned on by itself in the living room. My wife and son had already left for school and I was the last one to leave the house. The local news was on and I reached for the remote to turn off the TV. After I set the remote back down, I turned to leave. Hearing the news come back on behind me as I walked away was slightly jarring as, again, I was the only one in the house. I grabbed the remote again, pressed the Power button, and left. The TV did not come back on a second time.

One other time, while trying to fall asleep, something else interesting happened. I should probably note that I am a "back sleeper." My wife, however, sleeps on her side and, on this particular night, she had fallen asleep much faster than I. As we both lay still, I with my feet spread open at a natural and comfortable width, I felt something push the comforter down into the space between my feet. Our windows were closed and our room does not have a draft. I'd also been lying there for quite some time trying to fall asleep (to no avail by that point) and the covers by my feet had not moved or shifted over the ten or fifteen minutes prior. So when I felt this pressure by my feet, I was more than a little curious. However, so as not to alarm my wife (whose degree of fear of the paranormal is much greater than mine), I chose to ignore it.

I have considered conducting an EVP session in my own home, but based on what the real-life Teresa and Alix told the real-life Doug and Carla, which is that recognition of the activity often feeds it, I have not yet decided if I will do so. However, I'm sure that if I do, my wife will have something to say about it.

www.ingramcontent.com/pod-product-compliance
Ingram Content Group UK Ltd.
Pitfield, Milton Keynes, MK11 3LW, UK
UKHW041301180426
11947UKWH00009B/596